THE QUIET
MONSTER

CHLOE WRAY

A monster can come in many shapes and forms. A monster isn't always a nonhuman creature grotesquely deviating from a normal shape that children fear hiding under their bed.

A monster can have human qualities as well. It can be passionate but unsympathetic. It can be intelligent but manipulative. It can be strong but cruel.

What does your monster look like?

CHAPTER ONE

MARY AND SCOTT

Mary rushes up from her chair and bolts for the door of the classroom with her hand held tightly over her mouth. In a blur, she notices her classmates look at each other in confusion, while some laugh and roll their eyes. Mrs. Patterson continues explaining the syllabus for the upcoming Chemistry semester, not engaging in the distraction. Mary dashes down the hallway as fast as she possibly can without making eye contact with her fellow students running late for class. She stumbles around the corner, passing the gray metal lockers, and pushes open the girl's bathroom door, falling into the stall and heaving over the toilet. Her clammy hands hold the wall in front of her while she takes a deep breath, hoping she's finished.

After a moment, she sits back on her knees, wiping her mouth with several squares of toilet paper, embarrassed by the scene she just made. She slowly stands, walks out of the stall, and splashes water on her face.

With a heavy sigh, Mary looks up and stares at her reflection in the bathroom mirror. Her long, curly, red hair is pulled into a low ponytail, with stray curls escaping, falling onto her pale, freckled cheeks. She's unsure what made her nauseous and as she begins to mull over the possible cause, she feels an overwhelming sensation as she realizes she missed her period at the beginning of the month. For the second month in a row. The first month she didn't think much of it. Her friend, Susan, had missed her period before due to stress, so it wasn't concerning. As she wrestles with the facts, Mary is sure it must be a strange coincidence. She and her boyfriend Scott had only had sex once.

She takes several deep breaths as she tries to gain some composure. Her hands are still shaking and sweaty, even after washing them twice in warm water. Another student enters the bathroom, and they awkwardly smile at each other, then Mary contemplates what to do next. Go back to the classroom like nothing happened or go to the nurse's office and ask to go home for the day?

With her chin down, Mary lethargically walks out of the bathroom and heads toward the nurse's office.

"Good morning, Mrs. Campton."

"Hello, Mary. How are you today, my dear?"

"Not well. I was just throwing up in the girls' bathroom. It must be something I ate," Mary responds looking down at the floor, holding her stomach.

"Oh, I'm so sorry to hear that, Mary. Would you like to lie down in the nurse's room for a bit or would you prefer to go home? I can call your mother."

"I prefer to go home, thank you."

"Indeed, I'll call Ruth now." She hands Mary a pink absence excused slip. "Just leave this with your teacher, Mary. I hope you feel better soon."

"Thank you, Mrs. Campton."

Mary gets along well with the teachers and staff at her school. It's a small school, so everybody knows everything about everyone. Which has its positives and negatives. If you're smart, athletic, and make good choices, everyone is well-aware. If you struggle in school and cause trouble, there's no hiding it. Mary's junior class is all of thirty people. She fits in nicely, isn't overly popular nor extremely outgoing but not a recluse either. She and her best friend Susan have known each other since kindergarten. Mary wishes she could get Susan out of class right now and talk to her about all of this.

Mary leaves the nurse's office and heads to the chemistry room to grab her bookbag. She looks at her watch and notices that the bell will be ringing any minute, so she waits outside the classroom to avoid another scene. The bell rings and classroom doors fly open as students push through doorways, chattering on their way to the next class. Mary waits for everyone to leave, including Mrs. Patterson, grabs her bag, drops off the pink piece of paper on Mrs. Patterson's desk, and hurriedly leaves the room.

She tries to find Susan before the next bell rings and heads toward Susan's locker when she realizes her friend's next class is on the other side of the corridor. She'll never make it before the next bell rings. Mary adjusts her ponytail, sighs, and heads toward the front exit, where she knows her mom will be waiting for her.

The entry doors of the school are pushed open, and Mary squints from the glare of the late August sun as she spots the brown, wood-paneled station wagon parked across the street with her mom sitting behind the steering wheel, sunglasses on and windows rolled down.

Mary is sixteen and the eldest of five siblings. Four years younger than Mary is David. He and Mary have a typical brother-sister relationship—they argue constantly but will always have each other's back. Linda is six years younger than Mary and looks up to her big sis, following her around constantly, asking girlie questions and learning everything there is to know about boys and high school. Then there is Julie, who is ten years younger. While Mary loves the fact that

Julie looks like a mini-Mary, with her curly red hair and bright green eyes, she doesn't spend a lot of time with her. Stephanie, the baby of the bunch, turned two years old over the summer. With the wide age gap, and Mary's lack of interest in babies, they don't have much of a relationship, other than the occasional duty of having to babysit when her mom and dad enjoy an evening out. With friends and classes and boys, Mary is too caught up in her high school life to pay much mind to the hassle of siblings at home.

Ruth waves her hand from the station wagon, and Mary notices Julie and Stephanie in the back seat, looking at each other, Stephanie's hand in Julie's face. She hurries down the steps and crosses the street, squeezing behind the car. Taking a deep breath, she opens the car door. "Hi, Mom."

"You're not feeling well?" her mom asks.

"I think it's something I ate." The reply blurts out quicker than Mary realizes, with no time to think of how she wanted to answer.

"Let's get you home and in bed." Her mom smiles and rubs her shoulder.

The high school is only five minutes from home, and Mary's grateful that there isn't a lot of time for small talk. They pull into the long driveway that sits next to their gray, two-story, colonial home. Mary gets out of the car and opens the back door for Julie, who hops out and sprints into the house.

Her mom opens the door behind the driver's side, leans in to unbuckle Stephanie, and pulls her from the back seat. Mary leads the way to the house and holds the screen door open for everyone.

"Get yourself in bed and I'll bring up some 7-Up and Saltines for you," Ruth suggests.

"Thanks, Mom." Mary tosses her bookbag in the entryway and walks up the oak staircase lined with family photos. She closes the bedroom door behind her, crawls out of her school clothes, and puts on her pajamas. "Hi, John. Hi, Paul." Mary nestles her face into her two favorite living beings, sunning themselves on her bed—her two golden Persian cats, named from members of her all-time favorite musical group.

I wish I was a cat. You guys have it easy.

Mary buries herself under her floral bedspread, surrounds herself with her excessive number of pillows, and still finds no comfort. She lays there, just staring at the blank, white ceiling above her bed as tears stream down her face.

She is exhausted with emotions but tries to think about what to do next, although she wishes she didn't have this to think about. She flops on her side and contemplates talking to her mom. Mary has always felt like she could talk to her about anything. While her mom doesn't show a lot of outward affection to her children with loving words, hugs, or kisses, she is always there and supports each of them. It would be a difficult conversation to have; however, her mom would most likely be understanding and helpful in knowing what to do next. Mary also considers talking to Susan after school but realizes that if she does, Susan will have more questions and more worries about what to do. Like Mary, Susan is only sixteen, she's never been through this before either. After mulling it over and finding no better alternative, Mary decides to talk to her mom.

There's a gentle tap on the bedroom door and her mom slowly opens it as she carries the tray with 7-Up and Saltines. Mary rolls back over to face the door and her mother raises a brow when she notices that Mary has been crying. She sits on the corner of the bed, placing the tray on the floor. "Still not feeling well? Try a sip of this and a couple of crackers." Ruth offers her the soda and plate. Mary shakes her head and puts her hand up in front of the snack.

"I'm not hungry. And I don't think I'm nauseous because of something I ate. Mom, I missed my period. Two months in a row," Mary sobs as the words and their implication fall out. Her mother stares blankly, her mouth open, and no words come out. "Mom, say something!" Mary sobs even harder.

Her mother straightens her spine and inhales deeply. "I don't know what to say. I'm sorry. I wasn't expecting that at all. You need to give me a second to process the bombshell you just dropped on me." She turns from Mary and blankly stares at the wall behind the bed, clearly trying to remain calm. After a moment, she sighs and turns back to Mary, looking at her with gentle eyes. "You and Scott have only been together a few months. You're too young to be…"

"Stop, Mom," Mary impolitely cuts her off. "We only did it once, and we used protection."

"Well, you know that's not a hundred percent effective."

"I do now," Mary responds sassily.

"I'm grateful that you told me, you did the right thing." She rubs Mary's leg under the bedspread and softly mutters, "We need to find out for sure if you are pregnant. If you are, then we'll figure it out."

"Figure it out? Figure what out? I can't have a baby. I'm sixteen years old! I don't want a baby; I can barely help with Stephanie! And what about Scott? I know he loves kids and wants a family someday, but he's in college. He can't support us!" she sobs as more emotions roll through her.

"Slow down, Mary. First, we need to make an appointment with Dr. Ashton to find out if you're indeed pregnant. Scott is a respectful, hardworking young man who has been nothing but wonderful to you. I have no doubt that he will fully support you and a baby."

"Dr. Ashton? I can't go to him! He can't find out I'm pregnant before I tell Scott!"

"Then you'll need to have a conversation with Scott and tell him all of this. He deserves to know."

Mary had been dating Scott Ashton for only a couple of months. He's four years older than her, making the situation even more complicated. They had worked at Trails End Day Camp over the summer as camp counselors. Scott has such a love for working with kids, and he's incredible with them. This had been Scott's fifth year working at Trail's End, he'd started when he was a sophomore in high school, now a sophomore in college and home for summer break. It'd been Mary's first summer working there, the summer before her junior year in high school. For her, it was just a job, it wasn't about the kids. Mary and Scott had overseen the seven and eight-year-olds. Every morning, the kids would run up to Scott, jump on him, and hug every limb they could grab. Scott would take each kid, toss them to the ground, and pretend he was a monster chasing them into the woods. This was a daily occurrence the entire summer.

Scott and Mary had worked closely together, planning each of the day's activities. There'd been ten kids in their group, which was manageable for two counselors. He liked to make Mary laugh, and she'd picked up on the flirtatious comments he would make. At first, she thought he was just being polite, since their families were friends, and his dad was their family doctor. But each day, Scott seemed to be getting a little more friendly with her. He would gently rub her back as he explained his ideas for the activities and Mary would feel herself become flushed. She had always thought he was so handsome, with his piercing brown eyes, longer brown hair, and a smile that never went away.

Two weeks into summer camp, Scott had asked Mary if she wanted to take the canoe out after the kids left for the day. Mary had agreed. Every day from then on, Mary and Scott would engage in some camp related activity after the kids left, just the two of them. They would canoe, sit around the campfire, or go for a long hike. Each day, their feelings would become more intense, with more laughter, more touching, and more intimate conversations. Mary loved the attention that he gave her. Her favorite part of each day was after the kids left and she could just be with him.

The end of summer had neared, and it was the final week of day camp. While Mary wasn't going to miss her job, she felt an aching inside her that she wouldn't be able to continue seeing Scott every day. He would be leaving for college in two weeks.

One morning before camp started for the day, Mary leaned over the picnic table, arranging the place cards for the day's activities. She looked up and saw a bundle of sunflowers held in front of her, Scott behind them. The kids start giggling and cheering 'you have a boyfriend, you have a boyfriend.' Mary shyly smiled and kissed Scott on the cheek.

"Thank you, sunflowers are my favorite."

"I know, I remember you saying that. You said you love how they light up the bright blue sky. I have something special planned for us after camp today." Scott flashed the beautiful smile that made Mary melt inside.

"Oooh, a surprise?"

"I guess you could say that. Make sure you're hungry and we'll be out a little later tonight. Will your parents be okay with that?"

"Sure, I'll call Mom this afternoon and let her know." Mary sensed the excitement in her voice.

The day was spent on a nature hike. Scott led the group down the winding dirt trails through the thick woods. Glimmers of sun rays would peek through the trees. They were hunting for various plants, flowers, and berries based on the handouts each of the kids were assigned. After the hike, the kids sat at the picnic tables while they labeled and sketched their findings. Scott walked around to each of the kids, offering words of encouragement and answering any questions they had. The day was dragging for Mary. She couldn't focus on anything during the hike, and now she sat at the end of the picnic table, wondering what Scott had planned for the evening. It couldn't come soon enough.

Finally, the last kid was picked up from camp.

CHLOE WRAY

"See you tomorrow, Jason. Don't forget, you're in charge of bringing a box of macaroni. Tomorrow's craft day," Scott shouted. Jason turned and waved as he was running toward his mom's car, nearly tripping over the stump in front of him.

"Should I take you home now?" Scott smiled at Mary.

"Take me home? I thought you had a big surprise for me." She smirked.

"Stay here. I need to go to my car and get some stuff." He ran off and she sat on the top of the picnic table, her green sneakers resting on the bench. She brushed off dirt from her legs and readjusted her ponytail, wishing she had time to freshen up from being in the hot sun for several hours.

She watched as Scott returned with a small green cooler, a grocery bag, and a red and gray plaid blanket.

"Hmm, this looks interesting," Mary grinned.

"Welcome to Chez Scott. Tonight, I'll be preparing for you hot dogs over an open fire, corn on the cob, followed by everyone's campfire favorite—s'mores." Scott grinned and handed Mary a TaB. They tapped cans and took sips of the soda. "After our fancy dinner," Scott continued, "you will find the best entertainment this side of Omaha. You'll be immersed in a dark backdrop filled with the most beautiful constellations."

Mary's stomach fluttered. No boy had ever done anything like this for her. She was thrilled but didn't want to show too much excitement. She knew Scott was going back to college soon and didn't know what that meant for them.

"Why, thank you!" she declared. "I didn't know we had such fancy plans for the evening. I feel totally underdressed."

"You're absolutely perfect as is." Scott winked. He proceeded to start the campfire and pulled the hot dogs and corn from the cooler. He handed Mary a roasting stick, and they roasted their hot dogs trying to bat each other's off the sticks, leaning into each other, smiling, and laughing.

After stuffing themselves with s'mores, Scott laid out the flannel blanket near the campfire. He added more logs to the fire, then walked over to Mary and grabbed her hand, led her to the blanket, knelt down, and patted the ground for her to sit down next to him. Then he leaned in to kiss her. This kiss was different than their other kisses that summer. Scott held Mary's face, touched her hair, and pressed so hard but gently onto her lips. Mary felt lightheaded and her heart was racing.

"You know, I've never told anyone this before. In fact, I've never felt this way with anyone." Scott held Mary's hands between his. "I love you, Mary. This summer has been a blast. I've known you for years, but the way we connected this summer is something I've never experienced."

Mary didn't know what to say. She knew they liked each other and had fun together. She thought she loved him, but she really didn't know what love was.

"I love you too," she whispered. It felt good to say.

They continued to kiss and laid down on the blanket. Scott took off his shirt and caressed her. This wasn't his first experience with sex. She knew he'd had a serious girlfriend in high school, though they'd broken up when they both left for college. However, Mary had never been intimate with anyone. Scott was her first boyfriend.

He asked if this was okay, and Mary nodded.

The night sky glowed with stars, and they both gazed up at them, lying on their backs, arms and legs intertwined. There was no other place either of them would rather be, and they held on to every moment.

"What happens when you go back to school in two weeks?" Mary curled up into Scott.

"I would like to continue seeing you. Omaha is only two hours from here. I can come home every couple of weeks, and we can talk on the phone."

That's what Mary had been hoping he'd say. "Okay, I'd like that too. Mom's best friend lives in Omaha. Maybe I can ride with her sometimes. She can drop me off by you and pick me up after she visits her friend."

They smiled at each other, feeling confident that they could make it work.

Hesitantly, Scott suggested, "We should get you home."

"Yeah, I guess."

Mary folded up the blanket, Scott grabbed the cooler, and they walked to Scott's gold Ford Capri. It was an evening neither would forget.

CHAPTER TWO

I DO

Mary knows her mom is right. She needs to call Scott and let him know that she might be pregnant, though this is certainly a conversation that she prefers to have in person. It's Thursday and Scott has class until four-thirty. Mary looks at the clock on her nightstand, it's only one.

"I'll call Scott this evening, he's in class now. What do I even tell him?" Mary looks at her mom, feeling overwhelmed by it all.

"You tell him exactly what you told me. That you've missed your period, you're nauseous, and you think you might be pregnant. Let him know that you want to make an appointment with his dad and ask if he can be there with you. I'm sure Scott would want to have a conversation with Dr. and Mrs. Ashton prior."

They hear the door shut downstairs. Frank is home for lunch. He typically stops home for a quick sandwich halfway through his mail route.

"I'll go downstairs and talk to him. Or would you rather say something?"

"No, you can go ahead and talk to him. I'm going to stay in bed for a while."

While Mary knows that her dad won't be mad or angry with her, she doesn't want to disappoint him. Frank is the more affectionate of her parents, he's playful with each of the kids and generous with his big bear hugs and kisses. He tells each of his children how much he loves them every night before bed.

Mary thinks about having to call Scott and wonders what his reaction will be. She knows he's motivated and talks about his dreams of leaving Woodland Park to live in the city and teach underprivileged children. It's one of Mary's favorite things about him. He knows what he wants in life, and she can't even imagine what that feels like. Mary has never thought about her future or had dreams she couldn't wait to fulfill. If she is pregnant, she's not even sure if she wants the baby.

She wakes to a knock on her bedroom door, having dozed off while thoughts consumed her. Her dad peers past the door. "Can I come in?"

"Hi, Dad."

Frank walks in, pulls the desk chair over to her bed, and sits. "Your mom told me you weren't feeling well and came home early from school. She also told me you think you might be pregnant."

"I'm sorry, Dad. I don't know what to do." Mary starts crying again. "All of this is so horrible and overwhelming. I'm only sixteen! I can't have a baby."

Frank leans forward on the desk chair, his elbows on his knees, head in his hands. "You know that we think the world of Scott and the Ashton's. If you are pregnant, we will all figure this out and support you and Scott as much as we possibly can. First, though, you need to have a conversation with Scott and then see Dr. Ashton. We need to take this one step at a time."

"I'm not sure why you and Mom keep saying 'we'll figure this out.' It's me! I'm the one who will have to deal with all of this. What about school? I'm still trying to figure my life out. I can't even imagine having a baby now!" Mary shouts.

"I understand completely. You need to know that your mom and I are trying to be supportive. This will be a huge adjustment for everyone, yes, mainly you and Scott, however, you can't lash out at us. You got yourself into this situation, and we're trying to be there for you and assure you everything will be okay."

Mary turns on her side and stares at The Beatles posters plastered on her wall. Things seemed so much simpler just yesterday. She doesn't want to be burdened having to figure this out.

Frank stands, pushes the desk chair back under the desk, and holds his hand on Mary's back for a couple of seconds. He remains silent, leaves her room, and pulls the door gently closed behind him.

Mary immediately starts sobbing again. The tears coming from a place of anger and frustration rather than fear and worry. She turns back to look at her clock. It's now two-thirty. "God, can this day go any slower?" she moans under her breath, though she isn't sure why she wants it to speed up. She has a feeling of dread about having the conversation with Scott.

She reluctantly tosses the bedspread off and rolls out of bed, pulls a t-shirt and denim shorts from her dresser, and changes from her pajamas. David and Linda will be home from school soon and she doesn't want to draw any more attention to this situation right now. Mary stands in front of her bedroom window and looks out at the backyard, staring at the swing set and picturing her five-year-old self, swinging high with no care in the world.

With a deep sigh, Mary leaves her room and goes downstairs. Her dad has left to finish his mail route for the day, and Stephanie and Julie are in the living room, snuggled under an afghan blanket on the couch watching *Bugs Bunny*. Her mom is in the kitchen slicing apples, preparing the kids' afternoon snacks.

"Can I help?" Mary forces a smile.

"Sure, that would be great. Grab the peanut butter, please, along with the plates."

The front door slams shut, and David and Linda walk into the kitchen. They're both in Middle School, a ten-minute walk from home, so they typically walk home together. They leave the school with their friends, and as their friends reach their homes, it's David and Linda walking together at the end.

"How is everyone's day? Here, have a seat and enjoy your snack." Ruth sets the plates in front of the children.

"Thanks, Mom. The day was fine. I think I aced my Spelling test." Linda grins.

David answers with, "Fine," and proceeds to scarf down his apples and peanut butter.

"Julie, Stephanie, your snacks are ready," Their mom hollers to the living room. The girls come running, giggling and pushing each other out of the way.

The phone rings from the other room and their mom walks into the foyer to answer it. "Scott, hi, how are you?" Mary looks at the cuckoo clock in the kitchen and sees that it's only three-fifteen. She hears her mom reply, "I'll get Mary for you." She holds the phone to her chest, and peeks through the kitchen doorway, gesturing to Mary.

"Mom, can I take this on the phone in your room?" She wants to ensure she has privacy for the conversation that is about to take place.

"Of course, I'll wait for you to pick up."

Mary grudgingly proceeds up the staircase and walks down the hall to her parents' bedroom. She closes the door behind her, sits on the carpeted floor next to their nightstand, and rests her back on the bed. With a deep inhale, she picks up the phone. "I got it, Mom."

"Bye, Scott, you take care," Her mom says before hanging up the phone.

"I thought you were in class," Mary starts the conversation.

"My last class today was canceled, so I wanted to call you before I went to the library. I need to work on a research paper for my social science class. How's your day? I miss you!"

"I left school early today. I got sick during my chemistry class, so Mom picked me up."

"That sucks, I'm sorry to hear that. How are you feeling now?"

"I'm feeling better. I was in bed most of the day. Scott, we need to talk." Mary feels her hands shaking. "I wish I could talk to you in person."

"What's the matter? Are you ok?" She can hear the concern in his voice.

"No, I'm not okay. I'm not okay at all. I'm afraid I might be pregnant. I missed my period two months in a row and then I was sick this morning. I don't know what to do. We need to talk to your dad and find out for sure."

There is a brief pause. "Okay, I wasn't expecting that. We used protection that night at Trail's End. I know it's not always effective, but… Okay, everything will be okay." Mary can tell that Scott is shocked and can't articulate his thoughts. "I only have one class tomorrow and that ends at eleven-thirty. I'll come home after that. I can pick you up after school, and I'll call Dad tonight and ask what his schedule is like tomorrow afternoon. We should talk to him and Mom first and then ask him if he can give you a pregnancy test at his office."

Mary starts crying. "I'm so scared. I don't think I can do this."

Scott's voice changes to a soothing tone as he comforts her. "I wish I could hug you right now. I'm by your side. We love each other, and we will make this work."

Mary somehow makes it through school on Friday. She hasn't said anything to Susan yet. She wants to find out for sure and will then have a conversation with her. Mary feels that if she doesn't think about it or talk about it, maybe it's not true. She grabs the books she needs for the weekend and slams her locker shut, then she and Susan make their way to the front doors, shuffling through the sea of students ready to begin the weekend.

"Do you want to get together tomorrow and study for our history test? Maybe go to Frosty's for ice cream after?" Susan suggests.

"Yeah, maybe. Scott is in town this weekend; I think we have something planned with his family. I'll let you know though. Do you want a ride home?" Mary nods toward Scott, who's parked out front, standing against his car, hands in his pockets and smiling at Mary as he notices her walking out of the school.

"No, I'll walk. Thanks, though. I'll call you tomorrow." Susan waves to Scott as she leaves Mary and walks toward home.

Mary crosses the street, and Scott greets her with the biggest hug. He walks her to the passenger side, opens the door for her, and kisses her cheek before closing the door, then he runs back to the driver's side, hops in, and starts the car.

"I couldn't wait to see you. How are you feeling today?"

"Fine, I guess. I'm trying not to think about it until we know for sure."

"I talked to Dad last night. He only has two appointments this afternoon, so we'll go to my house now and he should be home shortly. Mom is there and she's looking forward to seeing us. I haven't said anything yet, I figured we should wait until we're in person altogether. Are you okay with that?"

"Sure, that makes sense. Will you do most of the talking? I feel sick to my stomach thinking about it."

"Of course. Mary, I was thinking all night about this, and, granted the timing isn't ideal, I would love to have a baby with you. We would have so much support from both of our families. I love children, I love you. I'm going to school for education. We can make this work."

Mary looks outside and stares at the passing trees. She doesn't share Scott's excitement or will to make this work. "Let's just start by talking to your parents and get the pregnancy test."

Scott pulls in front of his house and parks in the street. Mary looks up at the beautiful two-story brick home surrounded by pine trees. Scott's mom, Carol, is also a stay-at-home mom to their seven children. Scott is the third oldest. Mary sees Carol standing on the front porch, waving as they get out of the car, Scott and Mary walk up the sidewalk to greet her. Scott gives her a big hug, gently lifting her off her feet. Mary also gives her a hug. "Hi, Mrs. Ashton. So good to see you."

"Oh, I was so thrilled to hear that you were coming home this weekend, Scott, and that we get to spend time with you both. Your father is on his way home now. Come in, I just baked some chocolate chip cookies."

Mary and Scott follow Carol into the house filled with the intoxicating smell of freshly baked cookies. Scott turns around and they notice his dad pulling into the driveway. The three of them sit around the kitchen table, engaging in small talk. Scott's four younger siblings aren't home from school yet. Carol makes mention that they won't be home for a couple of hours yet. The two younger boys have baseball practice, and the girls are helping with the school play. The front door opens and John shouts, "Hi, everyone! I'm home!" Dr. Ashton enters the kitchen and kisses Carol on the forehead, while Mary and Scott stand from their chairs to greet him with a hug. "So good to see you both. How are you? How are your folks, Mary?"

"They're well, Dr. Ashton. Thank you for asking. They wanted me to be sure I told you hi for them."

"Hi, Dad. Thank you for coming home early today."

"It worked out well. It's a slow afternoon with patients. Besides, I would rather be visiting with all of you. Is there something that you both wanted to discuss?" Dr. Ashton pulls out a kitchen chair and joins them around the table as he grabs a warm chocolate chip cookie.

"Yes, there is. You know that Mary and I have been seeing each other for a couple of months, and we are very much in love. And we've been friends with the Thompson's for years. There isn't any easy way to say this, so I guess I'll just get to it. Mary thinks she might be pregnant. We know that we're both very young and it's earlier than we would like to start a family; however, I truly believe we can make it work. But before we even go down that road, we need to find out if she is pregnant. Dad, can you give Mary a pregnancy test at your office, so we know for sure?"

Mary just stares down at the table, her hands in her lap as she tries to control the shaking. She doesn't say a word. She doesn't know what to say.

Dr. and Mrs. Ashton turn to each other with a look of concern. "I have to say, this is not what I was expecting. Although, you both did the right thing by coming to us right away. There is nothing to discuss further until we know for sure that you are pregnant. So, yes, of course, we can go to my office now if you like. The results take two hours before we would get them back from the lab. Mary, are your parents aware?"

"Yes, they are. May I use your phone and let my mom know that we'll be going to your office?"

"Of course, dear. Go ahead, you know where it is." Carol points into the entryway.

Mary hangs up the phone and walks back into the kitchen. Scott and Dr. Ashton get up from the kitchen table. "Mom said she'll meet us at your office. She's leaving now," Mary says quietly as she continues to stare downward, feeling shameful and nervous.

"Okay, I'll drive us there," Dr. Ashton offers, and he, Scott, and Mary walk out the front door while Carol stays behind. The other kids will be home soon.

An hour later, they leave the clinic. Scott has his arm around Mary, and Dr. Ashton and her mom follow them out the door. "I should have the results in a couple of hours. I would think we'll hear something around six," Dr. Ashton lets the group know.

"Thank you, Dr. Ashton. We appreciate you squeezing Mary in for this." Carol grabs her keys from her purse while they decide what to do while they wait.

Scott turns toward Mary, "Do you want to come back to our house? We can go for a walk and try to get our minds off things for a while. Dad will let us know when he gets the call from the lab. Mrs. Thompson, we can come over as soon as we know."

"Let's just walk from here to your house," Mary suggests. All she wants to do is hide in bed. She doesn't want to be with Scott, Dr. Ashton, or her mom. She wants to bury herself in her pillows and blankets, snuggle up with John and Paul, and wake up from this horrible nightmare.

Carol gives Mary a hug and walks toward their station wagon. She and Dr. Ashton exchange goodbyes and pull out of the empty clinic parking lot, turning in opposite directions toward their homes. Scott pulls Mary close and holds her tight, his chin resting on her head. He kisses the top of her head and strokes her curly red hair. "Tell me what you're thinking."

"I think you know. I just can't wrap my head around any of this. I can't find it inside me to even be the slightest bit excited about the possibility of having a baby. Everyone keeps saying we'll figure it out, but maybe I don't want to figure it out. I feel like no one is taking my feelings into consideration and what this means for me. All the sacrifices that I'll have to make."

"You're right. I'm sorry you feel that way. I do understand that it's a lot to even imagine the possibility of being pregnant, let alone having a baby. I guess we're all trying to be positive about the situation and take it one day at a time." Scott seems to understand how difficult this must be for her, being only sixteen. He vows to her that he will be as patient as possible and hopes that if she is pregnant, she will eventually share his excitement as they work through everything together.

He gently grabs her hand, and they walk down the hill toward Scott's house. They're passed by a group of young boys riding their bikes down the middle of the street. They walk slowly together, not saying much of anything. Each of them processing their own thoughts.

"What time is it?" Mary asks.

Scott glances at his watch. "It's just after five. Would you like to keep walking or turn toward my house? We can hang out on the front porch until Dad gets the call."

"Sure, we can do that." Mary continues to stare at the sidewalk while they walk, noticing every crack and chip in the cement.

They turn down the street that Scott lives on and are distracted by the laughter of neighborhood kids running in sprinklers and playing kick ball. Mary envies them and the joy of not having a care in the world. She sees Scott's two younger sisters playing in the front yard as they approach the house, and Scott sneaks up behind them and gives a deep growl. They jump with excitement to see their big brother home for the weekend.

After some chasing in the front yard, Scott walks up the porch steps out of breath. He opens the front door and shouts,

"Mom, Dad, we're back. We'll be on the front porch," Then he and Mary sit on the porch swing, waiting for the call. They sit in silence, struggling with their own feelings of apprehension. Mary fears the results will be positive.

A short while later, which seemed like eternity, Dr. Ashton opens the front door and waves for Mary and Scott to come in. They follow him to the kitchen table, where Carol is already seated. "Kids, the lab called, and, Mary, you are pregnant. I guess, Congratulations. I understand this is going to be difficult to process and we have a lot to figure out, but we support you both and will help in any way that we can. We should go tell your parents."

Mary bursts out in tears and Scott pulls her in, rubbing her back and kissing her head. "Everything will be okay, Mary. I love you. We're going to have a baby. This is a good thing."

They arrive at Mary's house, she slowly opens the front door, and Scott and Dr. and Mrs. Ashton follow her in. They are warmly greeted by Mr. and Mrs. Thompson. "Come on in, everyone. I have coffee for us in the kitchen," her mom invites them.

Everyone sits around the table, unsure of who should begin the conversation. Mary feels it's her responsibility but can't find the strength to mutter the words. Scott begins, "Mr. and Mrs. Thompson, Dad heard back from the lab, and Mary and I are going to have a baby." Mary notices he can't help but smile as he says it.

Her dad breathes in deeply, running his hands through his hair, while her mom looks at Mary concerningly. Mary shows no reaction, just stares at the white tablecloth and empty coffee mug in front of her.

Her dad begins, "Okay, well, I'm glad we know. Mary, we understand this is difficult for you, being that you're only sixteen years old. Your mother and I support you, Scott, and this baby and will help in any way possible. I'm confident that the Ashtons share our feelings as well. We will all need to discuss what the future holds for all three of you. I'm sure that hasn't really been thought about at this point. Scott, you're excelling in your college courses and have about two years left. You need to continue and graduate. Mary, we'll discuss your options for finishing high school and decide on what makes the most sense for you."

Mary interrupts as a surge of fear floods her veins, "I can't do this. I can't have this baby."

"That's not an option, Mary. Both of our families are devout Catholics, not having the baby is not an option. You are in this situation and need to figure out how you and Scott are going to make this work for the three of you," her father replies sternly.

Mary pushes away from the table, sprints up the stairs, and slams her bedroom door. She falls onto her bed and buries her head between John and Paul. She wishes more than anything that none of this was happening.

"Mary, can I come in?" Scott softly requests as he cracks the door open. She remains snuggled between her two cats, not acknowledging him.

He enters quietly and sits on her bed, facing her back. John is startled and jumps off the bed.

"Sorry, John." Scott scoots closer to her and speaks gently. "Mary, I understand the fear and enormity of the situation. I'm terrified, too. I was just hoping that we could put all the unknowns and worries aside for at least a moment and embrace the fact that we are going to have a baby together. I love you, and I will do everything possible to make a good life for the three of us."

"I love you too, but I'm so scared, Scott. I don't think I'll be a good mother. I'm definitely not ready to be a mother." Mary's words are muffled in Paul's fur.

"You will be a great mother. Plus, we have both of our moms to help out." She feels him move from the bed, but he doesn't leave. "Mary, can you turn around. I want to see your beautiful face."

She begrudgingly flips over to face him.

He is beside the bed, knelt on his right knee, looking up at her. He reaches for her left hand and slides a royal blue hair tie that had been on her bedside table over her ring finger, twisting it several times to fit snugly.

"Miss Mary Lynn Thompson, you are everything to me. I love you so much and want to spend the rest of my life with you. Will you marry me?" Scott grins from ear to ear.

Mary quickly sits up; her eyes grow huge in delight as she holds both hands over her mouth. She suddenly feels less apprehensive and less alone.

"Yes, Scott, I will marry you," Mary excitedly exclaims as she throws her arms around his neck. *Everything will be okay.*

~ ~ ~

It's a sun-filled, stunning afternoon in late October. The colors of the maple trees are at their peak. Bright orange, yellow, and red leaves fill the cloudless sky. Mary peeks out the window from the bridal suite and sees Scott. She beams as she watches her soon to be husband. He looks so handsome, standing tall and proud in his tux, facing the rows of white chairs strewn with garland. The guests quietly chat with one another while they anxiously look around for the bride. Canon in D fills the outdoor air. Eyes become misty as women reach into their purses to grab their tissues. As the last note is played, Mary approaches the terrace, with her father and mother on each of her arms. They stop at the last row of chairs, and Scott smiles widely at Mary. She feels like a princess wearing a white, lace-covered dress with a matching floral, lace veil, her red curls falling over her shoulders. Mary smiles back at him, overwhelmed with emotions. She knows how lucky she is to be marrying Scott. It's been a challenging and stressful several weeks, but today she gets to marry the man she loves. Nothing else matters today.

The Wedding March begins, and Mary turns to look at her mom and dad. "Here we go." Mary is all smiles. They joyously proceed down the aisle, and Mary focuses on Scott the entire way. *This is happening. I'm about to become Mrs. Ashton.*

She kisses her parents on the cheek before they sit down for the ceremony, then turns to Scott. He takes her hands and holds them tight, leaning forward to whisper in her ear, "You look so beautiful. I can't wait to become your husband," then kisses her on the cheek. They stand under the ivy-covered altar, and Mary looks deep into his eyes, becoming lost in happiness.

After the heartfelt sermon, Scott and Mary exchange the vows they had written for each other. Both become emotional with what the other has prepared. The priest stands between them, and with a joyous smile, declares, "I now pronounce you husband and wife."

Scott grins at Mary and leans in to kiss his wife. "I love you, Mrs. Ashton."

"I love you, Mr. Ashton." She embraces him and couldn't be happier in this moment.

Guests applaud and cheer. Scott and Mary walk down the aisle, smiling and waving at everyone they pass by.

The evening is filled with dancing and laughter; they both wish it was never ending.

CHAPTER THREE

MICHELLE

Mary stands on the sidewalk and looks up at the white, two-story, clapboard house, while holding the last small box of her items. The early spring sun shines on her face as she walks along the sidewalk toward the house, avoiding the puddles from last night's rainstorm. Scott waves from the second-floor window and quickly runs out to grab the box from her arms. He kisses her cheek and takes the box. "Is that everything?"

"That's all my stuff. Mom and Dad are coming this weekend to bring the crib and help get the baby's room set up."

It's been six months since Mary and Scott were married. They had decided to wait until Spring to move in together since Scott was living in the dorms and needed to find a place for the three of them to live. After the wedding, Scott would go to Woodland Park every weekend to see Mary and spend time with her. While it wasn't ideal for most newlyweds, they knew their situation would create less than traditional circumstances. After many family discussions, Mary had decided to drop out of high school and get her GED. Although teenage pregnancy was becoming more acceptable compared to the late 1960s, she knew she was going to move to Omaha to live with Scott so they could raise the baby together. Mary has had months to process the thought of having a baby and has, for the most part, come to terms with it, with the help and support of Scott and both of their families.

Scott carries the box toward the front door, and they walk up the staircase to their first apartment together. She takes the stairs slowly, hanging onto the rail and making sure her feet touch each step. It's becoming harder and harder for her to move these days, and looking down at her feet has become an impossible task.

Scott opens the door and holds his hand out for her to enter. "Welcome home, Mary."

Mary looks around their new home as she stands in the living room, holding her hands over her belly. She breathes in the freshly painted walls, nodding in agreement of the color choice. They had looked at several apartments together and both had agreed on this one. It was within their budget, close to campus, and walking distance to a grocery store and park.

Leaning against the wall, she carefully kicks off her shoes, walks into the kitchen, and looks out the window into the backyard, where a monstrous oak tree towers over the house. Mary follows the hallway down to the small bathroom on the left and continues down the hall to the two bedrooms. The one at the end of the hallway will be the baby's room. She peeks in at the empty space then walks into the room next door, her, and Scott's bedroom. It's furnished with a queen bed that the Ashton's bought for them as a wedding gift. There is a small oak desk, a matching dresser, and a closet. Mary opens the closet door, where Scott's clothes are hanging on half of the rack. She didn't have much to bring, just her clothes and some personal items.

She turns to Scott, "Everything looks good. How were the first two nights here?"

"Great, but now it's home with you here. I met the neighbors downstairs, two young college guys. They seem like they'll keep to themselves. They've lived here for a year and really like it. Now, let's get you settled."

Her parents come that weekend to help with the baby's room. They bring the crib that Stephanie had used, along with other hand-me-downs. The baby is due May 11th, just a couple weeks away. They didn't want to wait any longer in getting everything ready. Scott and her father set up the crib, while Mary and her mom put the baby clothes in the dresser. They finish by hanging a Raggedy Ann and Andy crib mobile and a

Now I Lay Me Down to Sleep needlepoint. They look around the room, proud of their work.

"Perfect, the little one will love it." Her mom grins.

The due date is quickly approaching. Mary is getting more uncomfortable by the hour. She spends her days reading, taking care of the apartment, and making meals. She knows it doesn't make any sense to look for a job now since she'll be having a baby soon and will need time off. Scott spends his days on campus either at class, studying at the library, or at work. He picked up a part-time job on campus at the Children's Center. It's a daycare center for children of professors and students. The hours work perfectly with his class schedule. They're both feeling at home in their new place and with their new routines. Married life is good.

Mary often wonders what it will be like once the baby comes. *Will this new life still be great? Will Scott and I be as happy as we are now?* She's unsure if she's ready for the baby to come; however, she longs for the days when she can sit down without having to roll into position. She misses being able to move without a giant barrel in front of her. And most importantly, she can't remember the last time she got a full night's sleep.

Mary wakes up in the middle of the night to go to the bathroom. Again. At this stage in her pregnancy, she's going several times a night. She leaves the bathroom and feels a sharp pain in her lower abdomen, along with severe pressure in her pelvic area. The feeling is comparable to menstrual cramps but if they were delivered by a freight train. She hunches over, holding her belly, and feels her way back to the bedroom.

She uses her hand to leverage her body back into bed. "Scott, wake up. I might be having contractions." Mary reaches over and nudges Scott's back. The pain is unbearable. She has never felt anything so excruciating in her life. She curls up on the bed in a fetal position, rubbing her stomach. Moments later, the pain is starting to subside.

Scott is startled and turns to look at the alarm clock on the nightstand. "What? It's happening? Are you okay? It's two a.m.. Should we call your doctor or just go to the hospital?"

She feels another contraction coming on. "We need to go NOW." Her words are forced out with a moan of pain. Mary pushes herself up into a sitting position. Every passing minute brings sharper, more intense contractions.

Scott jumps out of bed, throws on his jeans and sweatshirt that were lying on the floor, and grabs the bag that they have packed and ready to go. He gently pulls Mary out of the bed and gets her dressed into her sweatpants and sweatshirt, holding her as they shuffle down the hallway, closing the apartment door behind them. The singing of crickets disrupts the nighttime silence. Scott opens her car door, helps Mary in, and shuts it before quickly running to the other side of the car, where he gets in and fumbles to get the key in the ignition.

He looks at Mary, "Are you doing okay?"

She nods.

"Let's go have a baby." Scott smiles, though with a trace of panic, while Mary rubs her stomach and takes deep breaths. The contractions are lasting longer and getting closer together. She is in extreme pain and trying to breath calmly through the contractions without screaming.

"We should try what we learned in our birthing classes. Remember?" Scott exhales in a pant-pant-blow pattern. Mary turns toward him and follows his lead. She breathes in deeply through her nose, exhales in two short pants, then one long blow, and continues the pattern.

While trying to focus on her breathing, she thinks about the last nine months and her struggle of accepting she was going to have a baby. She doesn't know if she's fully accepted the reality of it all or if she just got used to being pregnant and considered the baby bump more of change in her appearance rather than a human growing inside her. Nonetheless, the reality will be quite clear in a matter of moments.

~ ~ ~

"Come in," Scott responds quietly to the knock on the hospital room door.

Mrs. Thompson slowly opens the door, her smile beaming as she peaks her head in. "We're here to meet our granddaughter!" She's holding a giant stuffed rabbit with a yellow bow around its neck. She enters the room and is followed by Mr. Thompson and Scott's parents. He hugs each of them and then walks toward Mary as they follow.

"How is everyone?" his dad asks softly.

"We're all doing well. Momma and the baby were amazing. Once we arrived at the hospital, Mary pushed for a couple of hours and then we saw our little angel peek out. Mary didn't even need an epidural. The doctors were quite impressed." Scott turns to Mary, smirking proudly.

"Hi everybody." Mary tiredly smiles while lying in the hospital bed holding a tiny pink bundle. His mom leans over the bed, kisses Mary's forehead, and lifts the top of the pink blanket. The brightest, biggest blue eyes look up at her and everyone's hearts melt immediately.

"Everyone, meet Michelle!" Scott proudly announces as he introduces their beautiful baby girl.

CHAPTER FOUR

FIFTY

The sun is forcing its way out of the cloudy May afternoon. Mark holds up his wine glass and smiles at Michelle. "Happy 50th, Michelle!"

"How did that happen?" Michelle clinks glasses with Mark and he leans over to kiss her.

"Thank you, baby. I can't believe I'm fifty years old. That doesn't seem possible. I honestly feel like I just graduated college. Time goes way too fast. It's terrifying." Michelle sits back in her chair, taking in the beautiful view of downtown San Diego from the rooftop bar. "Crash Into Me" is playing on the outside speakers, and Michelle closes her eyes for a moment, grateful for this surprise birthday trip that Mark planned for her.

They had arrived the day prior. Mark told Michelle to pack a bag for five nights and to plan for warmer weather and a lot of walking. It wasn't until they arrived at the airport that

Michelle knew where they were going. She was beyond thrilled. California is her favorite place on earth.

Mark and Michelle have been married for eleven years, and he has treated her like a princess since the day they met. She had never felt a love like this before. In fact, she'd never felt deserving of it. She still doesn't. She had a history of making bad decisions with men and felt her world changed when she met Mark.

It was the second marriage for them both. Michelle has a son, Justin, with her first husband. She and Justin, who is twenty-five, are incredibly close, and Michelle is grateful every day for their relationship. Being a single mom for several years, a special bond had been created between them. Michelle also wanted to be a better mom than what she had growing up. She always put Justin's needs first as a child and enjoys quality time with him as often as possible. Mark and Justin are equally as close, he had raised Justin as his own child. He was the male role model Justin needed growing up.

The server approaches their table, and on her tray is a chocolate sprinkled cupcake with a glowing candle in the center. Michelle's eyes light up. "Yum! Thank you so much. You guys don't need to sing though." She winks at the server. Michelle focuses on the cupcake in front of her, inhales, and blows out the single candle.

"Did you make a wish?"

"I certainly did, but I can't tell you what it is or it won't come true. Let's just say it involves a winning lottery ticket."

Michelle and Mark finish their drinks and leave the restaurant. He takes her hand and asks, "Where would you like to go now, birthday girl?"

"Let's just walk around here for a while. I've always loved the Gaslamp Quarter neighborhood. Remember when we came here several years ago and went to the Farmers Market? We were buying so much food you would have thought we lived around the corner. It didn't even occur to us that we were flying back home the next day." Michelle laughs and rolls her eyes playfully.

"That was such a great time. We managed to eat most of that food before we flew back. Too bad there isn't a Farmers Market today." He nudges her with his elbow.

The sun has finally taken over the sky, and Michelle grabs her sunglasses from her purse.

"Not to bring up a sore topic, but can you believe my mom only sent a text for my birthday? It's my fiftieth birthday and my mom just sends a text. No card. No phone call." Michelle turns to look at Mark as she puts on her sunglasses.

"No, I really can't. But, then again, it's not too surprising knowing your mother. I'll never understand her."

Michelle and her mother, Mary, haven't spoken for over a year and a half. The last phone conversation involved Mary shouting to Michelle, "I can't do this anymore! I can't do this anymore! I'm tired of tiptoeing around you!" Then she hung up.

Michelle recalls staring at her phone in shock, her heart racing, completely confused by the outburst. During the conversation, Michelle had asked her mom what she meant about a snide comment she made about Mark. Her mom had replied "Oh, I think you're trying to pick a fight with me." Michelle shook her head and thought to herself, *I could have predicted that comment.* It was the standard statement whenever Michelle questioned something or had a difference of opinion.

She knows she did nothing to deserve that reaction or treatment, but she still feels a pain deep inside being treated that way by her mother. Although that behavior from her mom is nothing new, the hurt never goes away. The holidays passed with no greeting or acknowledgement from her mother, and it's now her fiftieth birthday and she received a text. Michelle received better birthday wishes from DSW.

Their relationship had been a lifelong struggle. They never shared that mother and daughter bond one admires in movies. Michelle always felt envious of her girlfriends' relationships with their mom's. They could go to them for deep conversations and advice on any topic. Their moms were their biggest cheerleaders and showed up at meaningful times. Even just shopping and getting nails done together would have been lovely. Michelle never had any of those things with her mom. It wasn't anywhere close to that. Her mom's priorities were 1.) herself, 2.) her second husband, Kevin (who is a total douchebag) and 3.) their sportsman's lodge that her mom and Kevin built themselves. Her mom spent more time caring for all the horses, dogs, and cats that they have at the lodge than spending any energy on her daughter. Michelle still isn't sure where she fell on that list of priorities. On second thought, she clearly isn't even on the list.

Michelle pulls Mark closer as they walk, resting her head on his arm, enjoying every second of her birthday trip but feeling a deep sadness and heartbreak that her mother once again didn't act like a mother on a special day of hers.

Michelle looks up at the sun, breathes in the California air, and reminds herself of all the wonderful people in her life. Her father being one of them. He, on the other hand, went all out for Michelle's birthday. He always did. Before Michelle and Mark left for their trip, she had received a package a day for a week from her dad. The gifts ranged from a tin of homemade cookies to a scrapbook of photos from when Michelle was a baby and toddler, along with jewelry and trinkets that Michelle had as a child and left at his house during their every other weekend visits together. The gifts and thoughtfulness meant the world to Michelle. She had no idea he had kept all those things from her childhood. Especially since they had lost twenty-five years in their relationship. Half of her life.

Michelle had reunited with her father only fifteen years ago. She had Mark to thank for that. A couple of years into Michelle and Mark's relationship, he had asked Michelle if she would regret not having a relationship with her father when, God forbid, the day comes that he's no longer around. That really hit home with Michelle, so she did some research online, found him, and reached out. She's so thankful to have him back in her life. It still pains her knowing she lost all those years with her father because she let her mom get into her head; the constant bashing of him and saying what a horrible person he is. Michelle was just a child; she didn't know any better, and one would like to think that you can trust your mother.

Darkness starts to fill the sky as the sun dips behind the buildings. "Should we get an Uber and head back to our room?" Mark suggests. They had been walking all afternoon. "We have a big day planned for tomorrow."

"That's right! The whale watching cruise. I'm beyond excited for that! Let's hope the whales will be active tomorrow. Sure, let's head back. My feet are killing me. We can get dinner at the hotel restaurant."

Mark grabs his phone and orders an Uber. Michelle turns toward him, raises her arms around his neck, gently kisses his cheek, her long wavy blond hair draped along her back, and pulls him in for the biggest hug. She holds on to him for at least a minute and whispers, "Thank you for the best birthday ever! I love you so very much!"

The next three days pass too quickly. Mark and Michelle enjoy each day with touristy adventures, sunshine on their faces, and lots of laughter. Michelle's eyes fill with tears as she zips her suitcase and pulls it from the hotel bed. "I can't believe we have to go home today. I feel like we just got here." She always gets emotional at the end of a trip. She loves making new memories and taking a break from reality.

Mark walks over to her, helping with her suitcase. "It's all good, we had an amazing time, and we'll be back. Besides, Charley is probably missing us." Charley is their adorable Corgi, also typically referred to as the best puppy in the world.

Michelle wipes her eyes and smiles. "Yes, we had an amazing time. Thank you again for the best birthday ever. That was so sweet of you to plan this. You're right. It will be good to see Charley. I miss the puppy kisses."

On the flight home, Michelle immerses herself in a Lifetime movie that she's seen twice already and finds herself thinking about her mom. Lately her thoughts are often consumed by her mother. She reflects over the fifty years of her life and finds it hard to process all the horrible things her mother has done, or not done. Until you remove yourself from a situation, it's difficult to see and understand how unhealthy something is. Michelle thinks to herself, *It's like the nursery rhymes we learned as children. Now as an adult, when you really listen to the words, they are terrifying.* She knows she needs to find a way to deal with all of this. It's been buried in her soul for far too long. She looks out of the window and stares at the sea of puffy clouds, breathes in deeply, exhales, and whispers to herself, "*I need to go to therapy.*"

CHAPTER FIVE

SESSION ONE

Michelle opens the glass office door and approaches a young woman with oversized glasses sitting behind a tall wraparound mahogany counter. "Hi, I'm Michelle Dupree, here for my one o'clock appointment with Dr. Tyson."

"Hi, Michelle, if you could please fill out this paperwork, Dr. Tyson will be with you shortly. You can have a seat over there." The young woman hands her a clipboard and nods toward the six chairs in a cluster by the wall.

"Thank you." She takes the clipboard and sits down in the slightly worn chair on the end, looking around the room before starting on the paperwork. She notices framed certificates on the wall, closed doors down the hallway, and children's toys in the corner by the front door. Michelle's heart is beating fast, and she wipes her palms on her jeans. She isn't new to therapy; she'd been to a few sessions years ago when she was married to her first husband. She feels it's different this time though, as she'll be uprooting painful memories from her entire life.

She looks back down and focuses on the forms. After filling out several pages disclosing personal and family medical history, she scribbles her signature at the bottom of the last sheet. Michelle gets up from her chair and places the clipboard on the counter. "Here you go. That should be everything."

"Thank you, Dr. Tyson will call you when she's ready."

Another patient walks in, and Michelle deliberately turns her head away and looks down at the floor. She feels a need to respect a certain privacy of others, as therapy is so personal, and it doesn't feel comfortable making eye contact. In any other environment, she would look at a stranger and smile. It just didn't feel right to do in this situation.

"Mrs. Dupree?" Michelle looks up and sees a tall, dark-haired woman, probably in her mid-thirties. She's wearing black slacks, a gray cardigan over a white top, and black walking shoes. Michelle is immediately comforted by her kind smile and warm brown eyes.

She stands and holds out her hand. The two gently shake while making eye contact.

She follows Dr. Tyson down the hallway and turns into the second door on the right. It's a large office, and the sun is shining through the two sliding windows. The first thing

Michelle notices is the long white couch decorated with yellow and white striped pillows. In front of the couch is a white coffee table covered in magazines and a Kleenex box. She sees a blue wingback chair facing the couch, and on the opposite side of the room is an L-Shaped walnut desk, with a floor lamp in the corner. Framed motivational posters hang on the walls. It's a pleasant atmosphere. Not like the dark, intimidating therapist offices on TV, with one brown leather couch intended for you to lay down on and pour out your heart and soul.

"Have a seat, Michelle." Dr. Tyson gestures toward the couch. "Can I get you a water?"

"Thank you. Yes, that would be great." Michelle walks toward the couch, moves one of the pillows to make room, and sits down. She places her purse on the floor and crosses her legs. Dr. Tyson sits in the blue wingback chair across from Michelle. She grabs her glasses and notebook from the side table.

"Thank you for completing the online assessment prior to our appointment. We always appreciate that. It sounds like you're having some struggles with your relationship with your mother. Is that why you're here today?" Dr. Tyson's soft and comforting voice helps to calm Michelle's nerves.

"Yes, that's correct. It's been a lifetime in the making, however, there have been things that have happened recently that made me decide I needed to talk about it. We had a falling out a year and a half ago and haven't spoken since." Michelle can feel her body fill with anger and hurt as she starts talking about her mother. "I have so much resentment built up toward her. Mostly due to the pain I have knowing my mom wants nothing to do with me. She never has, honestly."

Dr. Tyson nods and looks intently at Michelle. "Today I would like to start with talking about your childhood. Tell me what you remember about your relationship with your mother, your father, and anyone else of significance.'

Michelle uncrosses her legs and leans back into the couch. She grabs the pillow that she previously moved, places it on her lap, and hugs it. Any type of comfort now will help.

"My parents divorced when I was three years old. My mom and stepdad raised me, and I would visit my dad every other weekend. I truly enjoyed my weekends with my dad. Many of my favorite childhood memories are with him. We would always spend quality time together. I wasn't used to that with my mom. We would go camping, bike riding, roller skating, have picnics, play games, and on and on." Michelle feels a sense of ease as she reminisces about her childhood with her father. "One of our favorite things to do together was walk to the library and then get ice cream after, I would always get chocolate, Dad would get strawberry. I was a big fan of *Clifford the Big Red Dog*. We must have gone through all of those books several times at least." She grins thinking about their visits to the library. "He also taught me how to garden. We had a huge garden in his back yard. We planted lettuce, carrots, tomatoes, radishes, and a few other things in one half of the garden. In the other half we planted wildflowers. During spring and summer, we would spend so much time in that garden. I feel like we were always outside. Even in the winter. I had this red plastic snow block mold and we would make an igloo every year. We always enjoyed our time together." Michelle looks at the floor, smiling fondly.

Dr. Tyson looks up at her, "You have such special memories with your father. Do you share similar memories with your mother?"

"No, not really." Michelle pulls the pillow tighter. "I honestly don't remember doing much with my mom or even her being there when I needed her as a child. She did what she wanted to do. Mom remarried when I was young, to my stepfather Kevin. They were busy with each other. Since they would make plans that didn't include me, I also spent a lot of time with my grandparents and my aunt, who's a year older, Stephanie, if I wasn't by my dad for the weekend. Those were amazing memories too. No, I don't have any memories of quality time with my mom." She shakes her head as she looks across the room.

"Are you close with Kevin?" Dr, Tyson looks up from her notebook.

Michelle's skin crawls as she thinks about her stepdad. "No, not at all. He didn't care about me. He was all about my mom, which is fine, they should be in love, and he should treat her well, but it was different. It was almost bizarre and uncomfortable, more like an obsession. He never showed any interest toward me." She clears her throat as she holds her hands together tightly. "Looking back, I don't think he even liked me. He was in my life since I was probably five years old, and he has never told me he loved me. Oh wait, he told me once when he was drunk at my aunt and uncle's wedding, I was probably ten years old. He didn't even tell me, he was talking to some guests who referred to me as a cute, sweet girl and he said 'Yeah, she's great, I love her.' He also never told my son, his only grandson, Justin, that he loved him. Justin has always been a sweet and affectionate child, he would tell his grandpa 'I love you, grandpa' every time he saw him. Kevin would just pat him on the back and say, 'You too.' It broke my heart. I got used to him not telling me he loved me, but really? Your own grandchild? When it came to my mother, his hands were all over her constantly, and he told her he loved her several times a day."

"I imagine that was difficult for you. Especially knowing that he could show love and affection." She reaches for her mug on the side table.

"Exactly. It's weird, I was thinking the other day that you don't realize how messed up things are until you're removed from the situation and really reflect deeply on everything."

Dr. Tyson gives an understanding nod of agreement. "Tell me more about your relationship with your mother as a child. You said you can't recall a lot of special memories, that you shared those times with your father, grandparents, and Stephanie."

"That's right. Mom and I never spent any time together, just the two of us. It was always Mom and Kevin. They probably loved it when I was with my dad every other weekend. I wasn't in their way then." Michelle feels the pain of verbally communicating that her mother didn't choose to spend time with her. It's one thing to internally feel the hurt and loneliness. Saying it aloud impacts her feelings much deeper, making it even more real.

Dr. Tyson looks up from her notebook. "Did they work a lot or travel together, just the two of them?"

"Mom was a front desk receptionist for a nursing home and Kevin worked at the paper factory. They would both get home around five. So, starting in the third grade, I would walk home after school by myself, let myself in when I got home, make a snack, and do homework if there was any. They would come home after work, we'd have dinner, I'd watch TV, and then go to bed. Wake up. Repeat. As far as traveling, they didn't take big trips together, but they would go on weekend getaways, hunting, or boating, typically. Kevin is a big hunter, mainly white-tailed deer, elk, and turkey. His parents owned a cottage on the lake, and they would go there often with our German Shepard, Duke. They got Duke right before they got married. I would be with my dad or grandparents when they went. I swear they loved that dog more than me. They took Duke everywhere. Not once did they take me to that cottage." Michelle shrugs and forces a grin.

"That's the routine that you were accustomed to growing up?"

"It was for the most part until I was about eleven, maybe twelve years old. It was Mom and Kevin's dream to build a sportsman's lodge. A hunter's paradise if you will. They purchased thirty acres of land just outside of town, about ten miles. The property had a small lake, acres of hunting grounds, a couple loafing sheds, and an open area where they decided to build the lodge. They had casually looked for a year or two and were thrilled to find this property. They spent the next couple of years building the lodge themselves. The Back 40 Lodge is what they named it. It became their main focus in life. They would work their day jobs and at the end of the workday go directly to the property and work on the lodge. They did everything themselves. That also meant that I had longer days at home by myself." She brings her hands to her chest, pointing to herself. "Now I was also making myself dinners and typically going to bed before they would get home. There weren't cell phones back then, so I wouldn't know what time they planned on getting home. I just knew what time I had to be in bed, so I followed the rules accordingly." Michelle shook her head and looked up at the ceiling.

"Is it fair to say you looked forward to your weekends with your father?" Dr. Tyson looked at Michelle with an empathetic glance.

She nods and grins. "I did. He took the time to be with me. We enjoyed spending time with each other. However, those weekend visits stopped when I was probably thirteen years old. I became busy with friends, softball, and other activities that I needed to be around for. Dad lived forty-five minutes away. Looking back, I feel horrible that I stopped seeing him. It had nothing to do with him, it was just me being a thirteen-year-old girl, caught up in the life of her friends and extracurricular activities." She wishes she could go back in time and tell her thirteen-year-old self to figure it out and not give up the weekends with her father. "My dad continued to contact me though. I would receive a letter in the mail every Monday. I always looked forward to getting the mail on Monday after school, opening the letter immediately once I opened the front door. Ironically, he sends me an email every Monday now. And still, I look forward to opening that email every time I see it in my Inbox."

"Did you return your father's letters?" Dr. Tyson raises an eyebrow as she looks up from taking notes.

"I did. I would let him know how school was going, tell him about softball and all the other exciting things I had going on in my life." Michelle chuckles.

"Did your mother know about the letters?"

"I'm sure she did. I would have had to get stamps and envelopes from her."

"The snail mail letters continued until the wonderful world of the internet came about? Then he started emailing you?" Dr. Tyson smiles at Michelle.

"No. We actually lost contact for twenty-five years." Michelle's voice cracks, she squeezes the pillow tighter and looks at the floor, then grabs a Kleenex from the table in front of her as tears stream down her face. "I'm sorry," she whispers as she wipes the tears from her cheeks.

"Please don't ever apologize for tears." Dr. Tyson looks at Michelle reassuringly. "Take a minute and let's talk about that further when you're ready. Do you have any siblings?"

"I don't have any siblings. I'm an only child. I feel like my three aunts are like sisters though. We're close in age, especially Stephanie, being a year older, and we spent a lot of time together when I was growing up."

Dr. Tyson looks at Michelle inquisitively. "So, your mom was pregnant shortly after her mom, your grandma, had a baby, Stephanie?"

Michelle nods, raising her eyebrows. "Yes, that's right. Kind of crazy. Mom was pregnant at sixteen and had me at seventeen. I think that's part of the problem. I honestly don't think she ever wanted me. My grandparents were always very supportive of her when she got pregnant. Obviously, it wasn't ideal or the news they wanted, but they supported her. Grandma's youngest was just a baby, now her oldest was pregnant. I honestly think if it was up to only Mom, she wouldn't have had me." Michelle shakes her head and grabs another Kleenex and holds it tightly in her fist.

"That must feel awful. I'm thinking there are many reasons why you feel that way, and we will get back to that over the next several sessions. I want to go back to why you and your dad lost contact for twenty-five years. If you're ready to talk about that." Dr. Tyson turns the page in her notebook as she looks at Michelle empathetically.

"Okay." She breathes in deeply and finds the courage to continue. "Mom and Kevin were focusing all their time at the property and building the lodge. Weekday evenings, weekends, holidays, every spare moment. I would help on weekends if I didn't have any activities that I had to be at. One summer evening we were walking around the property. The three of us had spent the day clearing brush for where the parking lot was going to be. I was fourteen. I remember it being a hot summer evening, the sun was starting to go down. I just wanted to go home; we had been there all day. There wasn't a bathroom or anything on the property. Well, there was an outhouse. The outhouse was gross, I never used it. We would pack coolers for the day for food and drinks and go to the bathroom outside. I was hot, sweaty, and tired. I had an uneasy feeling. The three of us had never strolled the property after working all day." Michelle pauses. Her heart is racing, her palms are sweating. She's only talked about this twice before, to Mark and her aunt Linda. "Mom starts the conversation, holding Kevin's hand. 'Michelle, we need to talk to you about your father. We think you're old enough to know now.' I had no idea what they were about to say and felt a nervousness come upon me. I was also confused as to why she was saying 'we' and why Kevin was about to be a part of a personal conversation involving me and my father. 'When you were very young, a toddler,' Mom continued 'Your father sexually assaulted you.'" Michelle pauses again and takes a moment to breathe. "I stopped in my tracks. I didn't know what to say. I was embarrassed, shocked, and speechless. I never recalled any experience like that with my father." Tears fill Michelle's eyes, and she wipes them with the balled-up, sweaty Kleenex she's been holding onto.

"Take a minute, Michelle." Dr. Tyson holds the Kleenex box toward her.

Michelle deeply inhales then exhales and sits for a minute, processing her thoughts. She throws the used Kleenex into the trash can next to the couch and tightly hugs the pillow on her lap as it's the closest thing to comfort she has right now. She would love to ask Dr. Tyson for a hug but thinks that would be truly awkward and probably frowned upon.

"I started crying. I didn't know what to say or what to do. I didn't know what questions to ask." Michelle continues, "Mom didn't elaborate. I guess that was all that I needed to know, so she thought. I just needed to process it. I have no idea why either of them thought that Kevin needed to be a part of the conversation. That just added a level of discomfort for me. I'm sure he was there for Mom's moral support." Michelle scoffs and rolls her eyes.

"Was there ever any further conversation of the sexual assault by your father? Did your mom ever continue the conversation later or did you ask any questions that you had? Did she suggest getting you into therapy so you could work through something so tragic?" Dr. Tyson asks while continuing to take notes.

"No. I honestly didn't know what to ask. The whole idea of it was heartbreaking and hard to even process. I was afraid to talk about it. She didn't make any further mention of it after that evening. She never brought up the idea of therapy." Michelle leans forward with her hands clenched together on the pillow. "Looking back now, it doesn't make sense to me. If my dad sexually assaulted me when I was a toddler, why was Mom comfortable sending me to him every other weekend? It makes no sense at all. Also, I never had any uncomfortable feelings when I was alone with my dad. Kids are smart and have good instincts. Why didn't I feel uneasy with him and refuse to see him on my weekends with him? From that day on, I felt even more damaged. This tragic thing happened to me by someone I loved and trusted. Why did Mom wait so long to tell me? I had more questions than answers but knew I couldn't ever again see the man who did something so horrible to me as an innocent child. He continued writing the letters, but I didn't respond. Dad never stopped trying to be in my life. He never asked why I stopped communicating, and I never told him." She lets out a heavy sigh. "So that's why I wasn't in contact with my father for twenty-five years."

Michelle looks up at the clock on the wall. It's two, the end of their first session together.

CHAPTER SIX

REUNITED

Michelle gets into her car, rests her head on the steering wheel, and sobs. Fifty years of pent-up emotions pour down her face. She feels a sense of relief, along with anger and frustration and digs in her purse for a Kleenex, pulling out an empty pack. *You have got to be kidding me.* Her head is swimming with so many thoughts and emotions. She feels grateful that she took the initiative to start therapy but feels exhausted to have to discuss and relive painful memories, and she struggles with anger toward her mother for putting her in this position. These waves of emotions have been part of her daily mindset when it comes to her mother. Her heart and head swim with everything from sadness and confusion to hatred and disgust. How could her mother be such a narcissistic bitch? Even more infuriating is the fact that Michelle knows that her mom is playing the poor me, sympathy card to those few people she still has in her life. She can hear it now 'My daughter is so mean to me. She berates me and picks fights with me.' Her mom has always been the queen of gaslighting. Not just with Michelle but with her own siblings as well. Mary hasn't spoken to her siblings in several years. Michelle never really understood why, but the version she was always told was that Mary's sisters were bullies to her and she just couldn't take it anymore. Mary's final straw had been when their parents passed away and the siblings were working through the finances and there was a disagreement with how the money was being allocated. Mary had stopped all communication and blocked each of them. It was all confusing to Michelle, but being the loyal daughter she is, she supported her mother, which unfortunately meant that she also lost contact with her aunts, which was extremely tough for her. She'd been so close to all of them. It was like losing her own sisters. But she felt an obligation to her mother to support her. Once again.

Mary also treated Michelle differently when she stopped talking to her siblings. Michelle basically took on not only the role of daughter but also of three sisters. Mary was the closest to Linda, the next oldest daughter. They had been best friends. They talked all the time, visited each other, and took trips together with their husbands. Mary had shown sadness when she'd ended that relationship, but Michelle had always thought it was odd, as it was more from a victim's standpoint. As if Mary just couldn't believe how badly she was treated.

After the siblings' falling out, Mary would text Michelle every single morning at nine a.m. Every single morning. The texts were filled with a series of the same questions. How are you? What are your plans for the day? What is the weather like? How is Charley? How is Mark? How is Justin? The texts began to infuriate Michelle. No one's life is that exciting, especially to bomb text the same questions day after day after day. Her mom had hardly ever texted her when she was still talking to Linda. But every day, Michelle would respond to her mom with the same responses and the same politeness. This went on for several years, until Michelle and her mom stopped talking.

Mary and Kevin had also started inviting Michelle and Mark on vacation when the relationship with the siblings ended. That had been unheard of prior. In fact, Mary and Kevin had gone out of their way to not go on vacation with their daughter and son-in-law.

Michelle digs in the glove box, finds an old, not so soft, napkin and wipes her nose. She looks around the full parking lot, checks out her eye makeup in the rear-view mirror, and breathes in deeply. She turns the key in the ignition, pulls forward out of the stall, and heads home. Thankfully it's only a five-minute drive. She can't wait to get home and get a big hug from Mark and puppy kisses from Charley.

Michelle pulls into the garage and can hear Charley barking excitedly. She opens the door and is greeted with a kiss and a long hug from Mark, followed by wet puppy kisses from Charley.

"I'm glad you're home. How did it go?" Mark kindly looks at Michelle.

"I'm glad to be home! It went well for the most part. Of course, it's exhausting and difficult to bring up a lot of stuff, but I truly believe this will be good for me. Today we talked about my childhood and my relationship with my mom and dad. I really like Dr. Tyson, so that's a huge plus. She gave me some homework. She would like for me to try different breathing techniques to relax my brain when I become anxious and consumed with frustrating thoughts, which I think will prove helpful. My next appointment is the week after we get back from our trip to Florida."

"That makes me happy." Mark gives Michelle another hug. "I'm so proud of you for going. I understand it's not going to be easy, but I agree, I really think it will help you to talk about everything with your mom. Florida will be a good distraction also. Three more days!" Mark smiles widely.

"I can't wait! It will be so good to get away for a few days. Even though it's a work trip, we'll be able to squeeze in some fun stuff also. A change of scenery will be wonderful, and the weather will be much better than the cloudy, gloomy stuff we've been dealing with." She looks out the kitchen window at the rain hitting the backyard.

Mark and Michelle own an underground construction company. They've been in business for over ten years and have anywhere from fifteen to twenty crews continuously working for them. When they first started, most of their work had been in Nebraska, now Florida makes up most of their projects. They are grateful every day to be in business for themselves and to no longer work in the corporate world. They are also grateful to be able to travel to Florida on a regular basis to check on projects and spend some time enjoying the Sunshine State.

It's Friday evening, and Michelle pours a glass of wine. "How much longer before you're done for the day?" She peeks in Mark's office.

"I just need to send a couple more emails and finalize that the crews are ready to start on Monday. I'll wrap it up in about twenty minutes." Mark turns toward Michelle standing in the doorway.

"Okay, great. I'll meet you in the living room." Michelle kisses his cheek and leaves him to finish his work, Charley following behind.

She grabs her glass of wine, sits on the couch pulls her blanket over her lap, and turns on the evening news. Charley snuggles into his bed next to the couch, while Michelle stares blankly at the television, not paying any attention to what she's watching. She's feeling mentally drained from her session with Dr. Tyson.

"How much do you love me?" Mark walks into the living room and stands at the side of the couch.

"What do you mean?" She looks up at him, confused, then takes a sip of wine. A statement like this usually means Mark has something up his sleeve.

He sits on the couch next to her. "I reached out to Linda today."

Michelle's heart starts beating rapidly and her eyes swell with tears. "What? Why? Is everything okay? Did you talk to her?"

"I texted her at first, telling her right away that everything is okay with you and the three of us, so she wouldn't worry. I asked if she had time to talk. She said she was watching the grandkids and she would call when she got home."

Michelle wipes her eyes with the end of her sleeve. "This has been going on all day? Why didn't you tell me?" She is overcome with shock and gratitude.

"I wanted to talk with her first. She called back about an hour ago."

"How is she? How is everyone?" Michelle is completely overwhelmed with emotions and is trying to wrap her head around all of this. It's been years since they'd spoken, and the thought of having Linda and her other aunts back in her life is euphoric. When Michelle and her mom stopped talking, she felt such an emptiness. Michelle stuck by her mom when she stopped talking with her sisters, leaving her mom to be the only person she had a relationship with on that side of the family. Now she has no one from that side of the family.

"They're all doing well. I told her that you haven't talked with your mom in over a year and a half, and it breaks my heart to see you so hurt. She couldn't believe that your mom stopped talking to you and was pretty upset and disgusted by the whole thing. Especially considering she can relate firsthand. I also told her that you and I are going to be in Florida next week. She and Joe are at their Sarasota home until June. They would love to meet up with us while we're in the area."

Michelle puts her head in her hands and cries tears of joy. Mark goes to the kitchen to get her a couple of napkins, and when he returns, he leans over and rubs her back. "You're happy?"

Michelle wipes her eyes and blows her nose. "I'm beyond happy. Thank you so much, Mark. That is extremely kind and thoughtful of you. And, I'll admit, a bit risky. You didn't know how she was going to react. You are the best husband in the world. You have no idea how much this means to me. I already feel like a piece of my heart is back. I'm so grateful. I can't believe we're going to see them next week. It's been way too long. How do we even begin catching up?"

~   ~   ~

"Is that the place?' Michelle points out the rental car window to the yellow painted restaurant overlooking the ocean. Next to the restaurant is a Tiki bar surrounded by light blue stools. Every stool is occupied, and people cover the surrounding sand. Michelle is filled with excitement, knowing that in a matter of minutes she'll be reunited with Linda and Joe. She also feels slightly nervous and anxious since so many years have passed. She thinks to herself, *Will Linda be upset with me? Will it be awkward at first?* A variety of questions and thoughts spiral through her head.

"I think that's it. Yep, I see the sign, Shipwrecked. How are you feeling?" Mark senses some nervousness.

"Great! But also like I want to throw up. So much time has passed. I feel so bad that I let Mom get in my head and that I lost contact with them for all these years. My aunts have always been like sisters to me, and I lost those relationships for a significant period of time. I hope they're not upset with me. It makes me even more angry at Mom that she was okay with that. You know she loved it. She had control of me and didn't want me to have any involvement with them."

"I don't think they're upset with you. Based on my conversation with Linda, they're both very much looking forward to seeing you. We're meeting them at one. I'll find a place to park, and we'll walk over." Mark turns to Michelle and smiles.

She looks at the clock in the car, it's twelve-thirty. *We'll make it in plenty of time*, she thinks to herself. Mark finds a public parking lot and pulls into the last available stall, then they briskly walk the two blocks to the restaurant.

"Are they meeting us at the Tiki bar or restaurant?" Michelle's eyes scour the crowds of people dotting the beachfront.

"I think the Tiki bar." Mark walks toward the hostess. There's a high-top table next to the bar, and Mark and Michelle are seated there.

"Your server will be with you shortly." The hostess sets four menus on the table, smiles, and turns away.

"I'm going to go to the bathroom quick." Michelle looks around to locate the restrooms, then walks across the sand back toward the restaurant. Her hands are feeling clammy, and she can feel her heart beating fast. She's incredibly nervous but excited at the same time. In the bathroom, she looks in the mirror, takes a minute to get her composure, and leaves the restroom. She looks toward their table and stops. *They're here!* She sees Linda and Joe smiling and talking with Mark. Linda is wearing sunglasses, a khaki sun hat, and a light blue sundress. Joe is right next to her, sunglasses in hand, a baseball hat, a white buttoned-down shirt, and navy shorts. Michelle smiles, and all feelings of nervousness have fled. She walks swiftly toward them, reaching out her arms as she approaches the table. Michelle and Linda embrace and hold each other so tight as tears stream down both of their cheeks. No words, just happy tears.

"Oh my god, you guys! It's so great to see you! You both look amazing. You haven't changed at all." Michelle looks at Linda and Joe, smiling, lifts her sunglasses, and wipes her eyes.

"You both look great! You look younger than the last time we saw you. Mark, I love your beard." Linda gives Michelle another hug.

Food and drinks are ordered, and the conversation never stops. They talk about everything, from how Julie, Stephanie, and their families are doing, to the grandkids, and Justin's new job and apartment. At some moments, there are five conversations happening at once. Michelle's heart is full. They picked up like no time has passed.

Of course, Mary is the main topic of conversation. It's like unraveling the world's largest ball of twine. There are so many mistruths that come to light during the conversations. It's as if Mary was the quiet monster manipulating everyone close to her and creating her own agenda.

Michelle glances at her phone. "You guys, it's midnight! Can you believe it?" She looks around and sees two people sitting at the Tiki bar. The crowds of people have dispersed, and the moon's reflection shimmers on the ocean.

"What?" Linda looks at her watch. "You're kidding me. I feel like we just got here."

"I know," everyone says in agreement.

"And we barely scratched the surface. We could be here another week catching up on everything." Michelle laughs.

"I think we're going to get kicked out. It looks like they're closing the bar." Joe points to the bartender turning off the lights.

They get up from their stools and walk toward the front of the restaurant.

"Where's your hotel?" Mark looks at Linda and Joe.

"Just a block from here, across the street." Linda points in that direction.

"We'll walk with you then. Our parking lot is just past that."

They continue chatting about the remarkable day and how grateful they are to be reunited. Finally.

"Here we are. Mark, thank you so much for reaching out. I'm beyond thankful that you did. Today was amazing. We had so much to talk about, and it was definitely eye-opening." Linda hugs Mark goodbye.

Michelle turns to Joe and Linda, hugging Joe first. "Thank you so much for meeting us. It means the world to me to have you back in my life. It blows my mind that we've been told different stories by her for years. Now I'm questioning everything."

Michelle and Linda embrace one another. "I love you." Michelle kisses Linda's cheek.

"I love you too."

CHAPTER SEVEN

SESSION TWO

Michelle walks into the empty waiting room. No one is behind the front desk to greet her today. She sits in the same seat as she did for her first appointment while feelings of anxiousness fill her belly. *Why can't they play some upbeat music? Or any music at all?* The deadly silence doesn't calm her nerves, and she stares out the window into the colorless sky, longing for the sunshine. The gloominess takes a toll on her already fragile state of mind.

"Hi, Michelle! You can follow me." Dr. Tyson walks toward her office, steps aside, and follows Michelle in.

"How was your time in Florida?" Dr. Tyson hands Michelle a bottle of water and gestures to the couch.

The pillows are all on one side of the couch, not scattered like last time. Michelle sits on the empty side and grabs one of the pillows and holds it tightly on her lap. She figures it added a sense of comfort last time. She's now in ready position.

"It was amazing. We were busy with work but managed to find a little time to relax. The highlight though was reuniting with my aunt Linda and her husband Joe. I briefly mentioned my aunts in our first session. I haven't spoken to them in years, again, because of my mom. My husband Mark had reached out to Linda prior to our trip. Which was a total surprise." She smiles, so grateful that she has Mark and that he took the initiative to reach out to her aunt. "He knows I've been really struggling with my relationship with my mom, or lack thereof, and missing my aunts.

He reached out to Linda, explaining everything. She felt badly and understood what I was going through, as she'd gone through the same thing several years prior when Mom ended their relationship." She shakes her head in disgust. "Anyway, they have a second home in Florida, near where we were. So, we all met up for the day. It meant so much to see them and spend time with them. It was also an enlightening experience. We talked a lot about Mom and things that happened over the years. A lot of stuff didn't make sense, and come to find out, Linda and I had been told different versions of situations throughout the years. For example, Mom told Linda and the rest of the family that my dad put no effort into seeing me and that I would always get upset when it was my weekend with him. That's completely inaccurate. My dad never stopped putting effort in to see me, and I remember looking forward to our visits. It just makes me question so much when I look back at everything now. She lied to all of us for years about everything. Making up stories that made her look like the poor victim." Michelle is finding it easier to talk about her mom. She's not sure if it's due to her increased comfort level with Dr. Tyson or the confidence she gained in reconnecting with her aunts and sharing similar stories of lies and betrayal.

"It sounds like it was a wonderful visit and beneficial for those conversations to be had. As difficult as it probably is to learn about the deception, it's important to be made aware also. It will be healthy for you to have your aunts back in your life. Have you heard from your mom?" Dr. Tyson crosses her legs and leans back in her chair.

"I haven't heard from her. I honestly don't think I really want to. But I admit it's extremely hurtful. What kind of horrible person am I that my own mother wants nothing to do with me? I can't imagine not talking to Justin. There has been so much damage done, and to learn even more mistruths from talking with Linda and Joe, I don't want someone like that in my life." She holds her arm out in front of her at the thought of having her mom back in her life. "I need healthy relationships, people who truly care about me. I have so much resentment built up; I don't think I can ever be in a good place with her. She's put no effort into our relationship, ever. Ironically, that's what she said about my dad." Michelle turns toward the window and takes a sip of her water.

"In our sessions, we'll figure out what kind of a relationship you want with your mom, if any." She leans forward and looks at Michelle reassuringly. "It may be hard to have a relationship with her if there is a pattern of continuously being hurt and not feeling needed or loved. I understand you're not happy and you're probably mad about the situation, and that's okay. It's okay to not feel okay. That's a very normal place to be. There are five stages of grief; first, denial; second, anger; third, bargaining; fourth, depression, and fifth, acceptance. A person can feel each of them at different times or a combination of them."

Michelle thinks for a moment. "I would say I'm consistent with both anger and acceptance. Probably until the last few months I was in denial. I think I was in denial my entire life."

"That makes sense. It's important to remember that you will have different reactions and feelings as you work through the process. The reality is you lost your mother. Not by death, but you still lost your mother, and that will involve grieving, even if it's for the better not having her in your life. During our last session, I mentioned that I would provide a diagnosis for insurance purposes."

Dr. Tyson sets her notebook on the side table and walks to her desk. She pulls open the bottom drawer and takes out a manila folder. "Here's your file. I've diagnosed you with adjustment disorder with anxiety. Basically, it's a stress-related condition where you experience more stress than would be expected in response to a stressful event. That is to be expected considering what you're going through right now. Do you have any questions with the diagnosis?"

"I don't have any questions. It makes sense."

"Have you been practicing the breathing techniques we discussed last time?" she asks as she walks back to her chair.

Michelle nods, "I have. I particularly like the five-finger breathing exercise that incorporates using my left index finger and tracing my other hand, breathing in when I trace up a finger and breathing out when I trace down." She holds her hand out, tracing her fingers as she explains.

"I'm happy to hear that. We'll add that technique to your 'toolbox' then. As I mentioned last time, some things will work for you, some may not. Those that prove useful we'll add to your 'toolbox.' When you find yourself feeling anxious and unsettled, use a technique from your toolbox that you find effective. Hopefully we'll get to a point where you'll have several exercises to choose from." She smiles at Michelle and readjusts herself in her chair as she takes her notebook from the side table. "In our first session you mentioned that you feel like your mom might wish that she never had you, and today you mentioned feelings of resentment. Let's talk more about that." Dr. Tyson opens her notebook.

Michelle struggles on where to begin. "I do feel all those things. My mom was never there for me on a day-to-day level or at significant times in my life. I remember as a child having bad days at school, whether it was an argument with a girlfriend, a boy that picked on me, or a bad grade. You know, the typical things that a kid deals with. I didn't have anyone to talk to about that stuff. She was either not home or didn't want to be bothered by my problems."

"How did you handle those situations then when you were a child?"

"I just dealt with it. I remember feeling very alone and sad, but I would pretend to be happy and positive because no one was going to listen to me anyway if I had any issues or things I needed to talk about. There have been many times when I needed the love and support of a mother, and I could never count on her for that. I have to say one of the worst times was when I found out I was pregnant." Michelle's voice cracks, and she reaches forward to grab a Kleenex, sits back, and squeezes the pillow even tighter.

"I was twenty-four years old when I got pregnant with Justin. I was with my first husband, Scott." Michelle pauses and looks at Dr. Tyson. "Yes, I know, the same name as my father. Strange, right? We were dating at the time but had plans to marry. I called Mom to tell her the news, and she couldn't have been less supportive. 'You're what?' were the first words she muttered. It was a long time ago; I can't recall the exact conversation, but it was very quick. She couldn't get off the phone fast enough. I hung up, laid down on my couch, and sobbed. My own mother couldn't even be there for me at a time like that. Scott consoled me but had to leave for work. I called my best friend Sara to tell her the news. She was elated for us. After talking with Sara for a couple of minutes, she paused and said, 'Your mom,' as if the lightbulb instantly illuminated mid-thought. She knew that there would be an issue. She knew Mom and I always struggled with our relationship and that she had never been supportive of anything. I told Sara about the conversation, or lack thereof, and she immediately came over to be with me.

A few days later, I received a letter in the mail from my mom." She turns to look out the window as she feels herself become agitated. "We hadn't spoken since I shared the news on the phone of being pregnant. My stomach was filled with knots and my hands were shaking. I knew it wasn't going to be a congratulations on your birth announcement card. I opened the front door to our apartment, sat on the couch, and tore open the envelope. Inside was a two-page handwritten letter. She wrote me a letter telling me that I should have an abortion. She wanted me to have an abortion. Her daughter. Her daughter, pregnant with her first grandchild. The letter fell to the floor. I was in shock. My hands were shaking mad, my heart pounding through my chest. I couldn't believe it. My own mother told me to get an abortion. I was twenty-four, in a relationship, had a good job. I was well fit to be a wonderful mother."

Dr. Tyson's eyes narrow, as if in disgust. "That had to be difficult to hear, especially coming from your mother. That's an important time in your life that should be shared with your mom. Did you respond?"

She shakes her head and shrugs. "I did not. There was nothing to say. I was going to have that baby, and Scott and I were both excited. Scott's family was extremely supportive. I was grateful for that. I went to the city library, got books on pregnancy, read up on all of those, made a doctor's appointment right away, and figured things out without any help from her. To this day, I think she wanted me to have an abortion because she regretted having me. She was sixteen, I was twenty-four. That's a significant difference. She was in high school; I had a fulltime job. Her parents were supportive of her, mine were not. It still is just so unimaginable to me that she could be so callous, inhuman, heartless, insensitive. I could go on."

"Did you communicate with her at all during the pregnancy?"

"We went a period of time without talking. Again, it's almost thirty years ago, so I can't recall all the details. We were talking close to my due date. I remember that because when I told her the due date, her response was that they had guests at their hunter's lodge so they probably wouldn't be able to be at the hospital. Whose mom doesn't show up for the birth of their first grandchild?" Talking about this stirs up all sorts of emotions that Michelle had stored away for years. "I went ten days past my due date, so was scheduled to be induced. You would think having a scheduled date for the birth of your grandson may have been more helpful to work around, but they had guests for that date also." She takes a moment and swallows hard. "I had a very scary labor.

My first epidural didn't take, so I had a second one. I was pushing for hours. I had a nurse on each side of my bed. I was holding Scott's hand and squeezing it during the contractions. I had no idea I was capable of such force. His poor hand. I was pushing so hard I briefly blacked out. I shouted as loud as I could, which was barely a whisper, 'I can't push anymore.' My doctor stood at the end of the hospital bed, hands fully inside of me, and said, 'Keep pushing, Michelle.' I'm thinking *I just passed out, I physically can't do this.* Meanwhile, nurses were getting the room next to mine ready for me to have a c-section. Before the room was ready, I noticed the doctor gently pull out our baby. It wasn't the moment you dream of, with the doctor handing you the baby right away and kissing it for the first time. Our sweet baby, Justin, whose name we decided on prior, was immediately moved to a hospital crib and hooked up to a ventilator. I didn't know what was happening. I was exhausted. I couldn't see straight. I looked up at Scott, who looked panicked as well. The poor baby boy was bruised in the face and had punctured a lung during delivery." Michelle takes a few seconds to breathe and wipes her eyes.

"Justin was a brow baby; his neck and head were slightly extended, so it was like he was looking up rather than tucked down. His Apgar score was a two. I'm sure you know, it's based on one to ten, the higher the score, the better the baby is doing after birth. We couldn't hold him, which was so heartbreaking. I wanted to kiss him so badly and tell him everything was going to be okay. The nurses wheeled the crib with our baby boy down the hallway into the NICU. All I could do was cry. The doctor came back in my room and explained in detail what had happened and the next steps. I had trouble focusing on her, I had punctured all the vessels in my eyes from pushing so hard, so my vision wasn't clear. I had bloodshot eyes for days." She inhales deeply and takes a sip of water.

"I'm so sorry. It's absolutely traumatic." Dr. Tyson looks up at Michelle.

"We couldn't take Justin home for two weeks. When we left the hospital five days after he was born, we had to leave without him. I was devastated. It breaks my heart still thinking about how difficult that was. The entire experience was one of the most difficult things in my life that I had to endure." She feels overwhelmed with sadness reliving these memories. "You envision leaving the hospital with your new bundle of joy, putting him in the car seat, opening the front door, and welcoming him home for the first time. We went to the hospital every day to be with him. We had to take a CPR class at the hospital before we could bring him home just in case something happened with his breathing. But we got through it, and Justin is a happy and healthy young man today. You would never know the rough start he had to go through. That was one of the most difficult times in my life, and my mom wasn't there. She and Kevin came a few days later, once the lodge was free of guests. My aunts and their spouses all came the day Justin was born though. It meant the world to me. It was a two-hour drive for them, they rode together and stayed in a hotel. They would take turns coming into my hospital room when they were able to, and just knowing they were in the hospital was beyond comforting. It's even more frustrating because I know if my dad had been in my life at that time, he wouldn't have left my side."

Dr. Tyson lifts her glasses onto her head. "I'm happy to hear that Justin made it through and is healthy today. That had to be very difficult for you, experiencing something so tragic during a time that is supposed to be beautiful and joyous, especially without the presence of your mother."

Michelle nods in agreement. "It was, and that is just one of the many moments that I will forever be resentful for. She never came to help with Justin. A lot of my friends were having babies and their mothers would stay with them for a few days and help on a regular basis. I didn't get that. We couldn't even visit them after Justin was born because they had a 'no kids' policy at their hunter's lodge. Their lodge was more important than their newly born grandson and daughter. How do you get over that? It's even beyond resentful at this point. How can I care for someone or have respect for someone, not just someone but my mother, who blatantly disregarded me my entire life?"

Dr. Tyson gives Michelle a look of understanding. "How has the relationship with your mom impacted other aspects of your life over the years?"

"I've spent my entire life, including now, struggling with acceptance and confidence. I have very low self-esteem, which deeply affected me in school and relationships. When I was in grade school, I remember looking at classmates during class and saying 'hi' in hopes that they would say 'hi' back. Strange, I know. I always tried to be outgoing, and I think I came across that way, but it was forced. I'm constantly seeking approval and validation and do what I can to please others, even if it's putting my own needs aside. Even today I struggle with what people think of me and if I'm worthy of being loved or even liked."

"It sounds like you have a lot of people in your life who love you dearly. Do you question those relationships?"

"Sometimes." Tears stream down Michelle's face, and she holds the Kleenex to her eyes for a moment. "I have a hard time understanding that someone can love me for who I am." The tears fall harder, and Michelle tries to catch her breath. "I have such a fear of doing something wrong or disappointing people. Mark has really helped me through this, and I know he loves me unconditionally. I have never been taken care of or put first like he has done for me, and I still struggle with it. I don't feel like I'm deserving of it. I've gotten better, but I still have my moments."

"It's important to know that you are deserving of love, and people want to care for you and be there for you. If that's not what you were conditioned to growing up, it will be an adjustment, but you can work through it."

"I've been reading a lot about growing up with emotional neglect and being a daughter of a narcissistic mother. I've found some helpful ideas, but mostly I just become angrier and more frustrated when I read that stuff, so I'm taking a break and reading books for enjoyment instead as a distraction. There is one suggestion though that has helped me, the article said to look in the mirror at least daily and say, 'I love you.'" Michelle wipes her eyes again.

"Is that hard for you?" Dr. Tyson clearly senses Michelle's discomfort.

"It is. I know deep down I'm a good person, I just question what I'm deserving of. I have a lot of work to do for myself." She looks down at the floor and shakes her head. "I would have thought I'd have things figured out by the time I turned fifty."

"I don't think we ever have it all figured out, and that's okay. Be sure you take care of yourself and your needs. It looks like our session is over for today, we'll meet next week then. Continue those breathing techniques we discussed." Dr. Tyson stands, smiling at Michelle.

"Thank you. See you next week." Michelle smiles back and shows herself out. She walks down the carpeted stairs in the lobby that's shared by several other businesses and stops in the restroom. She washes her hands and focuses on the suds filling the sink, breathing in deeply. Then she looks up and stares at her reflection in the mirror. Strands of hair fall onto her face, her mascara is smeared, and her makeup is smudged. She manages to force a smile, looking deeply into her own blue eyes. "I love you," she tells the broken woman looking back at her.

Chapter Eight

Every Waking Moment

Michelle pushes open the front door. "Charley!" she playfully calls. "How's my puppy?" She kneels on the floor in the entryway to steal some kisses as he eagerly runs in circles, barking and sneezing. Charley sneezes when he's excited. He jumps up, his wet nose grazing Michelle's cheek, and she rubs behind his soft brown ears, kissing his head, grateful to be home.

As she walks upstairs, Charley bouncing behind her, she can hear Mark on the phone. She stands at the kitchen sink, takes a drink of water, and smiles out the window as she watches the neighbor kids bouncing and flipping on their trampoline. The June sun has finally decided to make an appearance today. Michelle gives Charley some more love and walks down the hallway to Mark's office. She peeks in, gives a quick wave, and smiles. "I'm home" she whispers, careful not to interrupt the phone conversation.

She continues down the hallway to their bedroom, takes off her summer dress, and changes into shorts and a t-shirt. Her head is feeling full, she just wants to be outside with the sun on her face.

Mark opens the bedroom door, asking, "How was your session today?" He leans in for a hug and kiss.

"We covered a lot. We started talking about some of the reasons why I feel resentful toward Mom and how my relationship with her has impacted my life and wellbeing. Of course, I had tears again. It's always exhausting to get it out there, but I can already feel myself getting in a better place. Do you have time to go for a walk? I need to get outside and clear my head. We can talk more on the walk."

"Absolutely. Just give me ten minutes. Charley, you're going to be so excited in just a few minutes." They both smile down at Charley.

Going for walks is the dog's favorite time of day. In fact, they can't say the word 'walk' without him going crazy. They have to say 'ww,' which is code for walkie walkie.

Charley leads the three of them out the front door, pulling Michelle behind on the leash. She looks up at the cloudless sky, closes her eyes, and breaths in, the sun on her face. Two robins are playing in the front yard, pecking their beaks in the grass in hopes of finding their afternoon snack.

Charley guides Mark and Michelle across the street to get to the sidewalk.

"You know, I've been thinking a lot about our visit with Linda and Joe. It's really been bothering me that we all have been told different stories over the years. It makes me doubt everything that Mom and Kevin have ever said. I feel like I don't even know who they are." They stop at the corner to let traffic pass.

"I agree with you. And to also learn things that they've said about us. It's as if they were playing different roles with everyone. Why? It's all so manipulative."

"Charley, heel." The eager ball of fur obeys the command, and they quickly cross the street. "Exactly. For instance, when Linda and Joe suggested to Mom and Kevin that they should invite us when they visit them in Florida and their reaction was, 'No, that's not going to happen.' Wow, that makes me feel great. I don't understand. What was their reason for saying that? You don't want to go on vacation with your daughter and son-in-law? But then they invited us to Florida after the fallout with her siblings. Why did they want to go on vacation with us then? It's all so bizarre." Michelle shakes her head and looks down at the sidewalk as they approach the park. She turns to see a group of young boys playing basketball.

"Yeah, I don't understand that. I would love to know their reasoning for everything. It's almost like they didn't want us all together for some reason."

"None of it makes sense. It has always bothered me that there is so much that I don't know about my childhood, especially when it comes to my dad. I felt like I could never ask questions since my mom hated him so badly. Mom never told me stories about me as a baby, or when it was her, my dad, and me. I don't know how they met. I don't know anything about the day they got married. What was I like as a baby? It's a lost part of my life. I want to know why my parents divorced. I was always told by Mom that she initiated the divorce because my dad didn't treat her well. Something in my gut is telling me I need to find out if that's true. More so now, considering we're learning so much of what we thought to be true isn't."

"That's a shame that your mom couldn't put her issues aside and talk to you about your early childhood years. I can understand why you're second guessing everything. Are you going to ask your dad why they got divorced?"

"No, I'm going to see if there's any way that I can get a hold of the divorce case. Do you think the county courthouse would have that? It's been over forty-five years. I'm not sure where to even begin."

Charley starts howling at a white fluffy Yorkshire Terrier coming toward them on the sidewalk. Charley is not dog friendly. It's his one and only flaw. Michelle pulls him to the grass and distracts him with treats until the dog passes.

"That's a great idea. I think calling the county courthouse would be a good place to start. If anything, they can steer you in the right direction."

They reach the end of the path, turn around, and head back home. "Okay, Charley, it's Daddy's turn to walk you now." Michelle hands Mark the leash, and they let Charley lead the way.

Mark looks over to the playground. "Are you going on the swing today?"

"Sure, there aren't any kids over there." They walk toward the playground, and Mark and Charley sit in the grass while Michelle swings. The swings have been one of Michelle's happy places this summer. She loves how free she feels with her toes pointing to the sky, her hair flowing behind her, and her legs pumping as hard as they can. She takes the time to be in the moment, focusing on all her senses. Her mind is free, even if it's just for a few minutes.

Soothed, she hops off the swing and they continue their walk home. Michelle chuckles to herself, she always loves the view when following Charley and his cute little Corgi butt swaggering with each step.

"Have you looked online lately to see if your mom and Kevin sold The Back 40 Lodge yet?" Mark turns to Michelle.

"I haven't looked in a couple of weeks. Last I saw it was still on the market. Can you believe it? It's been on the market for over two years. And they even dropped the price." Michelle tilts her head at Mark, squinting from the sun.

"Their dream of retiring somewhere warm isn't happening as soon as they wanted, I guess. They were vowing no more winters a few years ago."

Michelle shakes her head. "Yeah, I don't think they could survive anywhere else but there. That's where they are their happiest. No one to bother them in their perfect world. Just fellow hunters who keep to themselves or give them the utmost praise for creating such a paradise for them." She looks down and kicks a stick out of the way.

"They had a couple of families interested but 'they weren't the right buyers,' whatever that means. They should just be grateful to have some interested buyers. It doesn't matter what the new owners want to do with the place. They should just be concerned with selling it if their goal is to retire." Mark looks at Michelle, confused by the whole situation.

"Exactly. We even provided resources to them to help with selling. But they always have it all figured out and we're all just a bunch of idiots. It's too personal to them. They'll be there forever." She reminds herself it's not her issue anymore, even though she'd tried to offer help and suggestions so many times. "I was thinking about their house the other day. It always struck me as odd that they never had any family photos in the house. I understand that their home is an addition to the lodge but that shouldn't matter, it's not like patrons are coming in and out of their house. It's just strange. No photos of themselves, grandma and grandpa, you, me, or Justin. I take that back, I just remembered there is a photo of Duke on their desk in the office. Who doesn't have family photos in their home? I wonder what personality trait that's associated with."

Mark nods in agreement. "I always thought that was odd also. Their house is more like a hunting museum, very dark and drab. No personal touches whatsoever. Yeah, you're probably right. I can't see them living anywhere else either. They would be completely out of their comfort zone. Are we almost home, Charley?"

Charley's speed slows down as they turn on their road. His energy level is on empty compared to when they started the walk.

"That was wonderful! I always feel so much better after our walks." Michelle kisses Mark on the cheek as he opens the front door.

~ ~ ~

Ugh! Two a.m.?! Michelle turns her head away from the clock on her nightstand, rolls back over, and stares at the dark ceiling slightly touched by the moonlight. She is usually a deep sleeper. Not lately, though. Thoughts of her mom consume every waking and sleeping moment. She just can't understand why or how her mom can be this way, that she has made no effort to reach out. It's not even that Michelle wants her in her life, it just hurts terribly that her mom makes no attempt to have a relationship with her. Never.

Feelings of sadness, animosity, and disappointment fill her body. She recalls a breathing technique that Dr. Tyson suggested if she struggled with sleeping. Michelle envisions a place she would like to be right now; picturing a white sand beach butting up to the ocean where she can see into forever. She incorporates each of her senses, looking at sand for miles, a few people walking along the beach, white seagulls dipping into the ocean, the bluest of waters, and yellow and white beach chairs scattered around. She smells saltwater and sunscreen. She feels the sand under her feet, the ocean spray on her face, the sun in her hair, the smile on her face. She hears the waves crashing into each other, people talking and laughing, sea gulls chattering. Michelle is about to think of taste, when her eyes close, which is good timing because she didn't have anything for taste.

It's five a.m., and Michelle and Mark wake up to their alarm.

"Good morning, how'd you sleep?" Michelle rolls over to kiss Mark.

"Good. You?"

Charley jumps on the bed for morning snuggles.

"Fine. I was up for a while again. I had that dream that I keep having. Well, a different version but the same concept. My aunts and I were out for dinner, and we see Mom. She's wasted and alone. She was stumbling out of the bathroom at some restaurant that we were at. She sees us but keeps going. It's so strange I keep having dreams with her and she's always drunk and by herself. I wonder if that's some sort of premonition." Michelle wouldn't be terribly surprised.

"Wasted and alone, that could be the name of a new reality TV show. Seriously though, it makes you wonder, doesn't it? There's a reason why you keep having those similar dreams." Mark rubs Charley's head, who's nestled between the two of them. "What time should we leave for the game today?"

"I'm beyond excited. It's going to be a beautiful day to watch the Storm Chasers." Every summer, Mark and Michelle plan a weekday afternoon to go to an Omaha Storm Chasers game, Omaha's minor league baseball team. "Let's leave around eleven. The game starts at one, right? We can take our time getting there, walk around for a bit, and get something to eat."

"That works. Should we get up?" Charley hops off the bed, followed by Mark and Michelle.

~   ~   ~

Later that morning, they pull out of the driveway. "Bye, Charley, we'll see you soon!" Michelle waves to the house, then settles back and sighs. "So, I called the county courthouse this morning to see if they keep divorce records on file. She said they did; however, because my parents were divorced in 1976, the file is no longer at the county courthouse, I would need to call the Nebraska Historical Society. I called them and spoke with a woman who was extremely helpful. The files are kept at a different location than her office. She will send someone there tomorrow to see if they can locate their divorce case. I gave her my contact information and she'll keep me updated."

"I'm so glad you called. It sounds like it may be easier to track down than we realized. Hopefully you'll hear something soon."

"I agree. If they can find the case, I'm not sure what it would even include. But I'm sure it would provide some basic insight." Michelle looks out the window and takes in the view of the Omaha skyline.

"There it is!" Mark looks to the left, where cars are filling the parking lot. Crowds of fans wearing their Storm Chasers baseball caps and t-shirts shuffle in through the front gate.

"Let's go have some fun!" They smile at each other, ready for a day of sun, relaxation, and clearing their minds.

CHAPTER NINE

SESSION THREE

Michelle turns off the ignition and decides to stay in the car for a few more minutes. It's twelve-fifty, ten minutes before her session. The less time she sits in a deadly-silent, lonely, waiting room, the better. A group of young men and women dressed in business attire are walking into the office building. *I don't miss those days.* Michelle reminisces of her days in the corporate world, grateful to not do that grind any longer.

Her phone chimes and she grabs it, noticing an email from the woman at the Historical Society. The email is accompanied with a file attached. It's her parents' divorce records that she'd requested. Michelle quickly looks away from her phone and toward the office building. Her heart beats faster. *Do I look now? I can't look now. I don't have time for that. But depending on what it says, I may need to talk to Dr. Tyson, the timing could be great. But I suppose I already have enough to talk about.* Michelle puts her phone back in her purse and zips it closed. She hurries out of the car, shuffles between the parked vehicles, and briskly walks into the red brick building, worried now that she might be late.

She opens the office door and is greeted by the woman with the oversized glasses behind the front counter. Michelle notices a name plate reading Renee. "Hi, Renee, I'm here for my one o'clock appointment with Dr. Tyson." Just as she's finishing her sentence, Dr. Tyson approaches the waiting room. *Perfect timing.*

"Hi, Michelle, I'm ready for you." She smiles and walks toward her office. "How are you today?"

"I'm doing well, thank you." Michelle enters Dr. Tyson's office and walks toward the couch, takes her usual seat, and grabs her favorite yellow pillow. Her mind keeps going back to the email she just received. *Focus, Michelle. There's probably nothing you didn't already know in the documents anyway.*

"Have you had a good week? Is there anything new since our last session?" Dr. Tyson puts on her glasses and takes the notebook from the side table.

"It's been a good week. I'm still having trouble sleeping. Well, I fall asleep just fine, but then I wake up in the middle of the night. I did try that technique you mentioned last time. Imagining myself somewhere and incorporating each of my senses at that place. It has helped. I can never make it through all the senses before I fall back asleep." She grins as she recalls always falling asleep before she gets to the sense of taste.

"I'm so happy to hear that. It doesn't work for all my patients, so I'm glad you have found it useful. Some patients say it makes them more awake trying to think of a place and all the details involving their senses. We can add that to your toolbox as well then. Are you aware of what's causing you to wake up frequently?" Dr. Tyson looks up at Michelle inquisitively.

"Yes, I just keep thinking about what a monster Mom is and rehashing everything throughout my life. I've also been having dreams where the scenario keeps repeating itself. I dream I'm out with my aunts or Mark and I see Mom. Every time I see her, she is drunk and by herself. She always sees me but never acknowledges me."

Dr. Tyson's pen is flowing across her notebook. "Do you know what that could be related to? Has your mom had a problem with drinking?"

Michelle becomes uncomfortable, she has never talked about this with anyone. "I have memories from being a little girl and watching her get drunk frequently. When Linda and Joe got their first apartment together, they would invite Mom, Kevin, and their brother David and his wife Debra over on Friday nights. I would go along if I wasn't with my dad. I was probably nine years old. I remember sitting in Linda and Joe's living room by myself watching MTV. The adults would be in the kitchen, eating, drinking, talking, and laughing." She stares at the wall, trying to recall the details. "One night, I heard Mom crying in the kitchen. I was confused and concerned but didn't feel comfortable going into the kitchen to find out what was going on. I continued to watch music videos. Linda came out shortly after to check on me and I asked what was wrong with Mom. She told me that my mom had too much to drink. I didn't really know what that meant. I didn't know drinking too much would make you cry. I felt uneasy.

When we left that night, I got in the backseat of our white Oldsmobile Cutlass, and Kevin helped Mom to the passenger side. It was a struggle to get her to the car. He let go of her to open the car door and she couldn't stand on her own. She leaned over, about to fall, until Kevin grabbed her to keep her from planting her face in the pavement and then got her into the car. That happened a few times." Michelle notices herself nervously fidgeting with a string on her shirt. "There was a streak for a while that I remember feeling sad. To see one of your parents out of control as a child is extremely uncomfortable and worrisome. During that timeframe, I remember watching *The Carol Burnett Show*, and they would often do skits that involved a character being drunk and unable to walk. That was difficult for me to watch because it made me think of my mother falling-down drunk, which was not funny at all." Michelle takes a deep breath, exhales, and wipes her sweaty palms on her jeans.

"Those memories could very well be tied to the dreams that you've been having. Has there been any communication with your mother?"

"No, there hasn't been any contact. I don't expect anything anymore, and I've learned to accept that. And I have no intentions or desire to reach out." As difficult as it is, Michelle knows it's the right thing to do. It's the only way she can protect herself from continuously being disappointed and hurt by her mother. "I know that I'm in a much better place without her in my life. She's toxic and manipulative. A true narcissist who is incapable of showing compassion, empathy, and always finds a way to be the victim. Always. I just need to surround myself with people who truly love me and care for me. I need to make myself a priority and continue to practice self-love. And I need to keep seeing you, of course." Michelle grins.

Dr. Tyson smiles back. "In our last session we started talking about why you have resentment toward your mother. We talked about the lack of support when you were pregnant and when Justin was born. Are there other significant times in your life when you didn't feel supported by her?"

"Yes, definitely. Another significant time was when I married Mark."

"Did your mom not like Mark?" Dr. Tyson looks up from her notebook.

"She liked him. Well, eventually. When I first met Mark, he was going through a divorce. He and I took things slowly. I think that's why it worked out for us. We developed an amazing friendship before we got serious about dating each other. Obviously, he needed to get through the divorce before we could have a serious relationship. And, unfortunately, his soon to be ex-wife drug out the divorce for what seemed like forever. I think that was concerning to Mom and Kevin, but they wouldn't trust my judgment and would always create a different storyline in their heads. I could tell them the exact truth of what was going on, but they would then conspire and think they had a different reality figured out." Michelle is reminded of their self-righteous ways. It would often infuriate her. "This happened in so many situations throughout my life. I found out recently that Kevin would spend hours online trying to dig up dirt on Mark. Of course, he didn't find anything. After the divorce was finalized and they took the time to get to know Mark, they were accepting of him. I mean, Kevin was as accepting as he was capable of. He never went out of his way for anything or anyone other than Mom the almighty. Mark couldn't have been more kind or gracious to either of them."

Michelle readjusts herself on the couch, crossing her left leg over her right. She's more comfortable when she sits with both of her legs crossed under her, but she doesn't want her dirty sneakers on Dr. Tyson's pristine white couch.

"Mark asked me to marry him four years into our relationship. I knew early on that I wanted to marry him." She looks fondly down at her left hand as she touches her ring finger and twists her wedding ring. "I felt a connection with him like I never felt before. Mark truly cares for me and would do anything for me. I have never had that before, and it was challenging at first. I have always been extremely independent, so I felt guilty that he wanted to do these nice things for me and take care of me. I felt I didn't deserve that." She needs to continuously remind herself that she is indeed deserving. "Not only does he treat me amazingly well, but he and Justin have an incredible relationship also. They got along instantly. Of course, that was critical to me. I said 'yes,' and we started planning our wedding. Since it was a second marriage for the both of us, we wanted something smaller. We weren't going to have bride and groom wedding parties, and Justin was going to walk me down the aisle. Being that my dad was back in my life, we wanted him and Lori to be a part of our day also."

Dr. Tyson looks up from her notebook. "Your dad is back in your life at this point? When and how did that transpire?"

Michelle turns the pillow on her lap and pulls it toward her chest. "A couple of years into my relationship with Mark, he asked me if someday I would regret not having my dad in my life as I got older. I guess as both myself and my dad got older. That really resonated with me, and I was torn for a while. I grew up being told my dad was such a bad person. I was told he was awful to my mom. I was told he was horrible to me and did unforgivable things, we talked about that in our first session." She shrugs and shakes her head. "But I didn't have those memories. I decided I wanted to reach out to him and at least start a conversation. I found him on Facebook. He looked like more than twenty-five years had passed. It wasn't the face that I remembered as a little girl.

Dad was always a smoker. His face was worn and tired, showing the years that had passed by. It made me sad. I sent him a private message and he replied to me the next day. He was so appreciative and overjoyed that I reached out, and I knew I did the right thing." Michelle smiles with gratitude. "We communicated for several weeks and planned a Saturday afternoon to meet at the Farmers Market. It was me, Mark, Justin, Dad, and his girlfriend of fifteen years Lori. I love her, she's great. Dad got to meet his grandson for the first time, who was eleven years old then. It was wonderful. There were no conversations about the reasons for not communicating the previous twenty-five years. We just picked up from where we left off. From that day forward, we saw each other on a regular basis. Dad and Lori would come to all of Justin's baseball games and football games. We spent some holidays together. I was beyond thankful to have him back in my life."

"That took a lot of courage and strength to reach out after all those years. You should be proud of that, and to be grateful for your decision is even more remarkable." Dr. Tyson smiles at Michelle, looking up from her notebook.

"Thank you. Mom would disagree." Michelle smirks and gives a quiet chuckle. "When I called Mom to let her know that Dad was going to be at our wedding, it was one of the biggest fights we ever had. I remember Justin had a friend over and I was in the bedroom having this conversation with my mom, trying to keep my voice down. She was irate, livid, incensed, any other word to describe complete madness. I knew she wasn't going to love that my dad would be there, but she took it to a whole other level. She said 'he's your father by blood only, you need to call your grandma and let her know he'll be there.' I did later that day and she was fine. I'm not sure what that was all about. I told Mom she needs to get help if she is still this worked up thirty years later and can't be in the same room as her ex-husband. That's certifiable." Michelle feels her neck and face become flush. "They weren't even going to be in a room together, the wedding was held outside. The conversation went on for a while, probably over an hour, and it didn't end with any resolution or niceties. I was fuming and shaking mad when we hung up. I told Mark how it went, and he was appalled."

"You were hoping she could put aside her emotions for one day in support of you."

"Absolutely. No one enjoys being around their ex; however, you do what you need to in certain situations and be grateful that you've moved on and have a different life. Linda recently told me that the day Mom found out my dad was coming to our wedding she called her sisters and insisted they meet her that night for dinner. She was just so upset; she needed their support." Michelle rolls her eyes and shakes her head. "Mom told her sisters that she wasn't going to come to our wedding. Mom wasn't going to attend her own mother's funeral, so it's not terribly surprising she was planning on missing her daughter's wedding. Linda said she talked about it every single day up until our wedding."

"Did communication stop between you and your mom after that phone conversation?" Dr. Tyson holds her pen to her chin as she concentrates on Michelle's response.

"It did, I don't recall for how long though. Mom wasn't involved in any of the wedding planning, and I felt I couldn't share the fun updates with her. I asked Dad's girlfriend Lori to go wedding dress shopping with me. We had a great time and narrowed it down to three dresses. I asked Mom if she wanted to go with me to make the final decision." She looks down at her lap, still regretting that decision. "I guess I had some glimmer of hope that she wanted to be involved in her daughter's wedding day, not knowing that she wasn't even planning on attending. She and Kevin came for the afternoon. Mark, Justin, and Kevin went to a movie while Mom and I went to the bridal shop. It was awkward and apparent that she didn't want to be there. I pulled into the parking lot and before we get out of the car, she took out an envelope from her purse. She handed it to me and said it's from my dad's second wife. This woman tracked down my mom, wrote her a letter telling her my dad didn't treat her well also, and was asking my mom for advice. I was thinking to myself, 'What? You're showing me this right before we walk in to look at wedding dresses?' It still blows my mind." Michelle can feel her chest getting red. She can never hide when she's upset.

"How did you react?"

"I don't remember my exact words. I was shocked that she thought that was the best time to whip out that letter. I'm not saying my dad was perfect by any means. But my god, you need to move on. I wish I'd just pulled out of that parking lot and left. However, we went in, and it was as uncomfortable and disappointing as you could imagine. I didn't decide on the dress that day. I guess you could say the moment was ruined. I shouldn't have even asked her to come." Michelle pauses. "It just occurred to me. I wonder if it was even a legit letter or just another scheme that she and Kevin planned. Why would that lady write to my mom?"

Dr. Tyson leans back in her chair. "Well, that's an interesting perspective. I can understand why you would have second thoughts. I'm sure it was hurtful that your mom couldn't just be happy for you at that special time in your life."

"That's exactly it. Looking back, I don't know why I was surprised. I guess I just always hoped at some point she would want to be involved." Michelle shrugs.

"Did she attend your wedding?"

Michelle nods, "She did. Linda convinced her that she needed to be there. It wasn't until three days prior that she decided she would go. The family rented a van, they all arrived together. They didn't stay overnight at the hotel though; they drove back home later that evening. I guess it was enough for Mom to just show up for a couple of hours." She will never understand the wallowing self-pity of her mother. "Prior to the big day, I asked if she would join my best friend Jody and me in the bridal suite before the ceremony and help me get ready. She agreed, reluctantly, I'm sure. Especially knowing now that she wasn't planning on going to the wedding when I asked her. I just remember her sitting in the corner of the room, on a wooden chair, watching Jody help me with my dress. She looked absolutely miserable, like she wanted to crawl into a hole. She looked like she would have been happier with her skin on fire. She appeared that way the entire day. I found out recently that during our reception, my grandpa went into the hotel to use the restroom and ran into my dad in the hallway. They chatted for about twenty minutes. Mom saw them talking and was furious. She didn't talk to grandpa for weeks after that." Michelle thinks of her poor grandfather having to deal with that at the time.

Dr. Tyson pulls off her glasses and sets them on the side table. "In spite of everything with your mother, did you and Mark enjoy your wedding day?"

Michelle lights up. "We did. We had an amazing wedding day. The weather was perfect, I was marrying my best friend, and our son was part of our special day. There was so much love all around that day, she wasn't going to ruin it for me."

"I'm happy to hear that. Alright, Michelle, it was another good session. Continue working on the breathing techniques and the meditation that we discussed. We'll see you next week then."

Michelle sets the pillow next to her, grabs her purse from the floor, and gets up from the couch. "Great, thank you, Dr. Tyson." She walks out of the office, turns left down the hallway, and proceeds through the waiting room. "Have a great afternoon, Renee, thank you."

Now to look at that email.

CHAPTER TEN

TRUTH BE TOLD

Michelle quickly exits the building and rushes to her car. She considers looking at her email, but then tosses her purse on the passenger seat. She would rather be in the comfort of her home, just in case she learns something unexpected.

Once she arrives, she pushes open the front door, squeezing past Charley. "Charley, baby! How's my boy?" Michelle bends over and kisses Charley's nose, getting a wet sneeze in return. Mark is gone for the day at a job site, and she immediately heads for her office. "Charley, let's go downstairs."

Michelle walks into her sun-drenched office, sits in her white leather office chair, and opens her laptop. She feels a heaviness inside her. She's not sure what's she's anticipating or hoping to find or not find. Charley curls up into a ball on her feet as she nervously moves her mouse to the email from Andrea with the Nebraska Historical Society. The email thanks Michelle for processing the payment and states that a hard copy of the divorce case has been mailed as well. Michelle then moves her mouse to click on the attachment and waits for the ninety-nine pages to load. *Ninety-nine pages? That seems like a lot.*

She sips her water while she waits and bends over to rub Charley on the head. Finally, the document fills her screen, and she focuses in on the scanned and photocopied pages that are partly typed and partly handwritten. A stamped marking 'Clerk of Circuit Court Filed Jan 20, 1976' is in the center of page one. She scrolls her mouse to page two. Her eyes grow large and her stomach flips. *Scott William Ashton, Plaintiff vs Mary Lynn Ashton, Defendant.* Michelle's eyes move frantically across her computer screen. She continues scrolling through some legal verbiage until she sees what will contradict everything she thought to be true her entire life. *The defendant walked out on the plaintiff and their child as a direct result of her paramour relationship with Kevin Meyer.*

Michelle's eyes fill with tears as she turns from her computer. She pushes away from her desk, waking Charley, and hurries to the bathroom to grab a Kleenex. Her mind is spinning. She looks in the mirror as if to get a reasonable explanation. *My entire life I was told that Mom initiated the divorce because my dad treated her badly. She said she was a single mom for a couple of years. And Kevin, that pathetic soul, always touted that he'd waited years before dating my mom. He would say she wasn't ready for a relationship since she was recently divorced. Ugh, and we fed right into it. Aww, that's so sweet for you to be so patient, and now look at the both of you, so happy. Recently divorced? She was married! They divorced because Mom left me and Dad to be with Kevin. She left me and my dad for Kevin!*

Michelle's stomach is turning, she wants to throw up she's so disgusted. She leans on the sink, holds her head in her hands, and starts sobbing. Thoughts race through her brain. Nothing makes sense. She tries to think back as far as she can remember but can't focus on anything. She blows her nose, wipes her eyes, and takes a deep breath. *Mom and Kevin lied to me my entire life. Why? What sick, disgusting person can lie to their child about such a significant situation? And make my dad out to be the bad person? She left us! She told me my dad sexually assaulted me. But she left me with him? That can't be true either. I grew up thinking my dad sexually assaulted me. Does she have any idea how that fucked me up? I lost twenty-five years with my dad because of that.* Michelle becomes enraged. She can't find her breath. The more she tries to process this, the more infuriated she becomes. *My whole life has been a lie.* She sits on the bathroom stool for a few minutes and regains some composure, then feels an internal burning to continue looking at the divorce case.

She sits back down at her desk, pulls in her chair, and stares out the window for a few seconds. She needs to mentally prepare herself for any additional bombs she may uncover. Michelle turns toward her computer, rests her hand on her mouse, and continues to read. *Custody of the minor child of the parties, Michelle Kathryn Ashton, is awarded to the defendant subject to the reasonable visitation rights as to said child by the plaintiff.* Michelle whips her head from the computer. *She leaves me and Dad for another man and she gets custody of me during the Temporary Order? I'm guessing that's a sign of the times for the 1970s.* Michelle shakes her head and continues reading.

The plaintiff believes that the best interests of the child of the parties warrants a change of the Temporary Order so that custody is given to the plaintiff for the following reasons:

The paramour relationship of the defendant with Kevin Meyer adversely affects the welfare, health, and best interests of the parties' child.

That the defendant is not spending as much time with Michelle as would normally be expected and that the plaintiff can spend more time with the parties' child.

The defendant is not providing the child with a moral or religious foundation.

The defendant is searching for her own self-identity and satisfaction and is not as interested (as the plaintiff) in promoting the child's welfare and best interest.

Michelle smiles, feeling comforted that her dad was fighting for her and looking out for her best interests. She stares into the cloudless blue sky and tries to process everything that she's reading but knows she can't even begin to until she gets through the entire case. Michelle scrolls her mouse and continues. *Wow, after all that, the court ordered custody to Mom, with visitation rights to Dad until the case is final.*

Nothing is catching her interest. She continues to scroll through several pages of legal documents shared between the attorneys, then stops moving the mouse. *A letter from my dad's attorneys to the judge.*

Please find our petition and order for a Guardian ad Litem to be appointed to represent and protect the interests of the minor child of the parties, Michelle Kathryn Ashton. Michelle has heard that term, Guardian ad Litem, however, she wanted to be sure she understood it correctly. She opens a new tab and types *what is a Guardian ad Litem?* Resources and definitions fill the page. *Guardians ad Litem are professionals who are hired by the Family Court to represent a maltreated child's best interests in court proceedings. When the court is making decisions that will impact a child's future, the child needs an advocate whose sole concern is the best interests of the child for the duration of the court process.*

She clicks back to the case and continues reading. *Attorney John McVay would be suitable and a proper person to act as said Guardian ad Litem.*

Michelle looks up from the computer. *Attorney John McVay, I know that name.* Michelle drums her fingers on her desk. *That's right, I went to high school with his son, Dan McVay, who is now an attorney also. That's compelling. Small town coincidences once again.* Michelle shakes her head and scrolls further. She continues scrolling, staring blindly at pages of court schedules and counterclaims that mostly are above her head with all the legal verbiage.

She stops moving the mouse when she reads *Guardian ad Litem's Report and Recommendation Concerning Michelle Kathryn Ashton.*

The parties have one child, Michelle Kathryn Ashton. The blond four-year-old seems to be alert and intelligent. On both occasions I saw her she appeared to be happy and well behaved. Michelle quickly scans the overview of the home visits; both went equally well. She continues reading and her eyes stop when she sees *Intangibles – Mary: She seems concerned with Michelle and Michelle seems well behaved and happy with her. There is, however, already someone else in Mary's life. And it appears she is not as oriented toward Michelle as Scott is.*

Mary leans forward in her chair, completely fascinated by this information. She pushes her hair behind her ears and continues.

Intangibles – Scott: An unannounced visit to his home found him working with a group of his students making a terrarium. It was obvious that he works well with small children. In his living room he had numerous pictures of Michelle; so many, that a sincere feeling of love and concern for her was apparent. In my discussions with him he constantly referred to Michelle, his visits with her, and her future.

Michelle looks up from her screen, smiles to herself, and wipes her eyes. His love for her is so clear just from reading this alone. She lets out a big sigh and continues to read.

Recommendation: I am confident that either of these parties could give Michelle a proper upbringing. A balancing of their negative characteristics is unproductive. Upon balancing their positive characteristics, Scott's education and work geared toward helping small children, his edge in both current and future stability for work and relocation as well as the feelings he generates that he would more fully dedicate and gear his life around Michelle lead me to conclude that Michelle's best interests would be served by having her custody placed with Scott.

Michelle rereads the recommendation and is confused. *If the Guardian ad Litem recommended that my dad have full custody of me, then how did Mom get custody?* She furrows her brow and scrolls further to try and piece it all together.

Petition and Order for Psychological Evaluation. That sounds intimidating. Michelle scans the document and focuses on the third bullet point.

3. The facts brought to the Petitioner, the Guardian ad Litem, leads Petitioner to feel that complete psychological evaluations of both parties would be necessary for the Court to make its findings pertaining to the best interests of said child. Wherefore, Petitioner requests for an Order directing Douglas County Unified Counseling Services to conduct a complete psychological evaluation of both above parties and to make information available to Petitioner and the Court.

Michelle deeply inhales and turns from her computer. *What facts were brought to the Guardian ad Litem to urge him to request a complete psychological evaluation for both of my parents?* She struggles to process everything in front of her. A document that is nearly forty-five years old. A document that is revealing so much information about her childhood that she is learning about for the very first time in her life. She had no idea there was a custody battle that lasted well over a year. Despite what she was always told, her dad tried everything in his power to be involved in his daughter's life. *Dad wanted me more than Mom. What happened?*

The next page shows the assets for each of the parties. *Here it is. The letter from Douglas County Unified Counseling Services with the results of the court order for the psychological evaluations.* Michelle sits up in her chair and slowly reads every word in detail.

It should be stated that neither party was very critical of the other, and both parties appeared to be genuinely concerned about the welfare of their child. Both parties were fully cooperative throughout the evaluations, and both seemed to be quite straightforward and honest in the responses given to questions asked. Both were also rather obviously tense and anxious throughout their respective evaluations, despite all efforts made to put them at ease. Since both participated so well in the interview type of evaluation, it was not felt that the administration of formal psychological tests would add anything of significance.

In this evaluation, Scott was seen as being somewhat more rigid and compulsive and as perhaps having the stronger need for achievement in life. Although he is likely to be a success vocationally, he may have some difficulties in his interpersonal relationships, in large part because of his need to be dominant or in control of the relationship. Michelle is taken aback by what she's reading. *There is also some question as to his ability to get truly close to other individuals. As a father with custody of the child, he would likely be very responsible and dutiful in carrying out his parental obligations, but he might at times tend to be a little too rigid or demanding in this endeavor, just as he is with himself.*

Michelle gets up from her chair and paces her office, processing what she just read. *I would love to know what was involved in these interviews. It seems like quite the conclusion to be determined in such a brief meeting. What do they even mean by that? More rigid and compulsive? Aren't rigid and compulsive words with opposite meanings? Difficulties in interpersonal relationships?* She shakes her head and watches a woman outside walking her brown Dachshund and is grateful for the distraction. *Now for Mom's evaluation.* She sits back down at her desk.

Mary struck the examiner as being somewhat more emotionally responsive than her husband, and she was perhaps somewhat more flexible and less demanding, both of herself and those around her. Her considerations for the child tended perhaps to be somewhat more global and less detailed than were those of her husband. She was seen as thoughtful and responsible in her considerations regarding the child and there was no question about her willingness or ability to be a good parent.

Michelle looks up at her office wall. *That's it? It hardly seems like an equal assessment. How do they even come to these conclusions? This report is almost the exact opposite from the Guardian ad Litem's report.* Michelle shakes her head in confusion and continues to read.

Neither party demonstrated any serious emotional problems, and both were seen as being concerned and responsible individuals. It did appear to the examiner that Mary has considerably more interest in eventually centering more of her life on home and family than would Scott, and in the long run this might be the healthier situation for the child.

What?!? Michelle moans out loud. *Eventually centering more of her life on home and family? Eventually? No consideration for leaving me and my dad and the efforts that Dad was showing constantly. The more I read the more confused I become.* Charley looks up at Michelle with an empathetic head tilt. Michelle is filled with frustration but knows she can't stop reading now. *A home study was also done? This custody battle went on forever.* Michelle pulls her chair closer to her computer.

Regarding his marriage, Scott states 'Lack of money was a problem, but we did survive and realized that someday we would be well off and not have to worry about money. Another problem we faced daily was the fact that I was going to school and Mary was employed, the parental roles were reversed in our family. I assumed that Mary thought that my education would be the best for us and didn't think she objected too much, considering what it would be like in the future. Her work was hard, I know, and this did require us to spend less time together as a family but someday it might have been better.'

Michelle is touched. *Aww, Dad. He was going to school to provide a better future for his family. Going to college isn't easy, especially getting your master's degree. Dad also had a steady income from the GI bill. Mom was upset about having to work? Everyone makes sacrifices in a marriage. I wonder if that job is where she met Kevin.* Michelle continues reading.

Scott believes he is closer to Michelle than most father-daughter relationships. He views his relationship with Michelle as that of a parent by offering discipline, leadership, understanding, assurance, and guidance and a relationship of a friend by giving companionship and the opportunity to communicate with and be accepted by others. Scott states that in the past and present he has had a deep interest in Michelle's development as a happy, intelligent youngster; whereas he believes Mary has not always shown interest nor taken enough time to play and be with Michelle.

Scott provided the following reasons why he believes Michelle's best interests would be served by being in his custody. '1.) I believe that my future presents a brighter future for Michelle. I am employed and hopefully will only go up. Mary is currently uncertain of her future with plans to attend community college in the fall. 2.) With my background in psychology, sociology, and counselor education, I feel that I have much more to offer Michelle. I also have an educational background in many other areas. 3.) Because of Mary's relationship with a male friend, she once again shows that she cannot take all the responsibility of a single parent. 4.) I, as a parent, can discipline Michelle in a positive manner rather than constant punishment. I do and will encourage Michelle's good behavior.' Mr. Ashton is concerned about how seriously his attempt to get custody of a female minor child will be viewed by the court. He states, 'I'm currently working as a house parent for 18 girls and I'm becoming very aware of things that Michelle might face in the future.' His long-range plans for Michelle would include the opportunity to participate in activities through school, church, and Girl Scouts. He also wants her to have a college education; he is buying US Savings Bonds for this purpose.

Michelle gets up to stretch her legs. She walks upstairs to refill her water bottle, Charley closely following. She thinks sarcastically to herself, *Yeah, Dad wanted nothing to do with me and put in no effort whatsoever.* Michelle is deeply moved reading everything he did in an effort to gain custody. *Now to read Mom's portion of the home study.*

Mary believes that Scott should have found work while attending school to help support the family and should have been more concerned about the family's financial planning. She stated that prior to their separation, he frequently was moody, had temper tantrums when things didn't go his way, and occasionally hit her. Mary said 'I told him our marriage was in danger and that I just couldn't take much more. I'm not even sure he heard me. He never seemed to listen or take me seriously.'

Michelle taps the mouse and looks down at Charley. *Why is this the first time she ever mentioned my dad not treating her well. She's had plenty of opportunities, over a year, during the entire divorce and custody process. It makes no sense. If that was the case, this probably would have been wrapped up in a matter of weeks.* She scrolls further down the page.

Regarding the custody of her daughter, she said 'there are many good reasons why I think Michelle would be much happier and better taken care of if she lived with me. One reason is that

I'm Michelle's mother. A mother and daughter can share many more activities and similar feelings together. I think I'm more capable of understanding her because we are both females.'

Michelle scoffs and rolls her eyes. *Wow, that's compelling.*

She has a good home with me. She is well taken care of, plenty of food, clothes, a nice home and neighborhood, and lots of love.

Michelle turns her head. *Seriously. That's it? You think you should have custody because we're both females and you provide a roof, clothing, and food? I thought that was the law.* Michelle is irritated, but not surprised, by the lack of compassion and willingness to do anything for her daughter.

Ms. Ashton is dating Kevin Meyer and said that they plan to marry after her divorce. They met in May 1975 when they both worked at the vehicle manufacturing plant.

Michelle slams her hand on the desk. *I knew it! She met Kevin while Dad was going to grad school and she was working. Unbelievable. How long were they dating before she left us?*

She turns back to her screen and looks intently at the next several pages, which appear to be notes from the actual court dates, six months after the order for the psychological evaluation. Michelle squints to read the handwritten details of the hearing. *Why can't this be typed out?* The handwritten paperwork lists the people who testified on the plaintiff's and defendant's behalf. *How come there aren't any details of the testimonies?* Michelle would have loved to know what was said on both her mom and Dad's behalf. She gets through the names of those who testified.

Still struggling to read the handwritten notes, she focuses in on what seems to be the end of the hearing. *Court hears arguments by both sides and Guardian ad Litem. The court makes findings and awards custody of the minor child to defendant subject to reasonable visitation rights by plaintiff. The court grants defendant an absolute divorce on the grounds of cruel and inhuman treatment. The court enters judgment divorcing the parties of this action.*

Michelle's heart stops before it begins pounding through her chest. *What?!? Cruel and inhuman treatment? You have got to be kidding me. My dad treating her badly wasn't brought up until months later, not until the very end. And never anything about my dad hurting me or sexually assaulting me. None of it is true. None of it.* Michelle is overcome with feelings of hatred. *The two people that I was supposed to be able to trust the most fed me hellacious lies since I was a little girl. I'm guessing grandma urged her to get custody of me as it was the right and responsible thing to do. You can tell by the case notes that she didn't go out of her way to get custody. She was just following the motions. I'm confident that Mom was disappointed with the outcome. She didn't want me. She never did. I'm sure they're grateful to finally be rid of me.*

She keeps scrolling through the few remaining pages of invoices and letters between the attorneys. *What are these?* Michelle stops moving the mouse. *Notes that Dad included with the first several child support payments to the clerk of courts.*

Please find the enclosed check for child support payment for Michelle Kathryn Ashton. Michelle is at my home this weekend and we are having a very good time together. Even though Michelle only comes up on weekends, she has made many friends here.

Helping Michelle Grow, Scott Ashton

Please find the enclosed check for my daughter's child support payment, Michelle Kathryn Ashton. I am mailing this check before the actual due date. I want to give my child everything I can. I'm very concerned about the future of our child. I believe that the parent separated from the child has many more duties toward the child rather than just the monthly child support payments. These other duties are to let the child know that you still love them, and the child is not responsible for what is happening between Mom and Dad, and to see the child whenever possible.

A Very Concerned Parent, Scott Ashton

Please find enclosed check for my daughter Michelle Kathryn Ashton's child support payment. Michelle and I have been spending as much time together as Mary (Michelle's mother) lets us, but there does not seem to be enough time to do everything we would like. Michelle and I are inseparable, we mean so much to each other, and no matter what happens this will always be true.

A Very Concerned Parent, Scott Ashton

Michelle takes off her glasses, sets them on her desk, wipes her eyes with her sleeve, and rests her head in her hands. That was a lot.

CHAPTER ELEVEN

MOVING FORWARD

Michelle stares out the window, watching as the green, rolling farmlands pass in the blink of an eye, becoming a blur in the distance. She sees her smile in the reflection of the truck window and feels content and grateful for the amazing weekend they just spent with her aunts and their families.

"It's a good day for a drive." Michelle looks at Mark and stretches her arm out to rub the back of his neck.

"It couldn't be better. I'm glad we got an early start though. I always feel like the six-hour car ride typically takes us close to eight hours, with all your bathroom stops and everything." Mark grins and winks at Michelle.

"Ha-ha, funny, but yeah, you're not far off." Michelle playfully slugs his arm. She turns and looks behind her to find Justin sleeping in the backseat and Charley in his bed on the floor, snuggled in his favorite blue blanket, also sleeping. "We wore those two out this weekend." Michelle laughs.

Michelle's phone chimes, and she reaches into her purse to find a text from Linda "It's Linda. Aww, it's a picture of her with Julie and Stephanie making sad faces. It says, "Miss you guys already," with a kissy face emoji. How sweet is that?"

Mark smiles at Michelle. "I love it!"

"That was such a great weekend. It was absolutely wonderful to see everybody and spend some quality time with them. It means the world to me that everyone took the time out of their busy schedules this weekend to spend it with us and plan such fun things. I honestly can't believe that it's been over five years. It makes me so sad to think about everything that we missed out on during that time. I get so mad at myself for letting Mom get into my head. I've lost years of relationships with those who mean so much to me, who truly love me and would do anything for me. My aunts, my dad. It's a shame."

"It really is. I'll never understand why she's like that. She's going to be a lonely old woman someday. Well, we did have a great weekend, and it was so good to see everyone. It's been way too long. Nathan and Noah are young men now. I think they grew two feet." Mark smiles at Michelle.

"I think she's a lonely old woman now." Michelle shakes her head. "I know, they've grown so tall! And Anna, kicking butt in college. She's a junior? Crazy!"

"It's great to see everyone doing so well. It's heartbreaking that we missed out on so much those five years. I'm happy for Ben and his recent promotion. He's been with that same company for a while now. I love his dog, Bella. Of course, Charley had to be a little jerk puppy with him." Mark shakes his head and grins.

"And Joe and Linda's grandkids. So sweet! They're such good kids. Jason and Morgan have their hands full with three kiddos under five years old, but you can tell they're great parents. It melted my heart when Connor dropped his piece of pizza on the ground, looked around thinking 'don't make a scene, people,' picked it up and went back to eating it. He handled it better than I would have." Michelle chuckles.

"How about when Jenna walked up to me and said, 'Wipe my face.' I was like 'What, honey?' 'Wipe my face.' 'Okay, I'll wipe your face.'" Mark smiles widely.

"She's so precious. We made a lot of great memories this weekend. And new traditions. We'll be sure we make a trip to visit every summer. My heart is full again having them back in my life. When I think about my relationship with my mom, it was very lonely and unfulfilling. I'm in such a better state of mind now. No more listening to her snide comments about me or supporting her when she's victimized once again. No more being her scapegoat. In one of the articles that I read about how to deal with a narcissistic mother, it said to remove yourself from the relationship and live your best life. That is exactly what I'm doing now, and it feels fantastic. We're almost to Justin's house. Let's grab lunch before we have to drop him off." Michelle looks in the backseat, where Justin is still sleeping hard. She rubs his knee to wake him up and he hesitantly opens his eyes.

"Good morning! You crashed hard. We're almost to your place. We'll get lunch before we take you home. How does Chinese sound? The restaurant down the street from you has outdoor seating so we can take Charley."

Justin stretches out his arms and yawns. "Sure, that works. I slept the entire ride? Dang, I must have been tired. You guys, it was such a fun weekend. I loved seeing everyone."

"I know. We're so glad you were able to take time off work and join us. It was so great to spend a long weekend with you." Michelle looks through the head rest, grinning at Justin.

"Alright, we're here." Mark pulls into a near empty parking lot.

Michelle steps out of the truck and bends over to stretch her legs, slightly moaning. "It feels so good to get out and move. I can't sit for that long. This body is getting old."

Mark grabs Charley from the back seat, rubs his face in Charley's neck, and puts him on the pavement. The pup walks to the back of the truck and immediately relieves himself on the tire.

Justin slowly slides out of the truck, still waking up. Not paying attention, he steps right into a large puddle from yesterday's rain shower. "Dammit," he shouts, shaking the water off his black slides. He throws the wet socks in the back of the truck and jogs to catch up with Michelle and Mark.

"I'll take Charley and get a table over there if you guys want to go in and order. I'll have my usual, General Tso's chicken with white rice. Thank you." Michelle takes Charley and they walk to the round white tables covered with red umbrellas. "Charley, it looks like we can have any table that we want." They choose the table closest to the door, and Michelle ties Charley's leash to the bottom of her chair before taking a seat.

After a few moments she points to Mark and Justin walking out of the restaurant toward her and Charley with two trays of food and drinks. "Here they come, Charley. Is that Daddy and Justin? Thanks, guys. It looks delicious. I'm starving now."

"You're welcome. It's nice that we have the place to ourselves." Mark sets the tray on the table and sits on the red stool.

"Here you go, Mom." Justin hands her the Styrofoam container with her General Tso's chicken, rice, and a fortune cookie. "You didn't want anything to drink?"

"No, I have my water. Yay, a fortune cookie!" Michelle doesn't hesitate to open it and reads the message out loud. "You are exactly where you're supposed to be." She smirks and looks up at Mark and Justin. "Well, isn't that fitting. We just had a great weekend with family that we haven't seen in years, and I'm with my two favorite people. I'm saving this fortune." The three exchange smiles of comfort.

They eat their Chinese food and share stories from the last couple of days. No one wanting the weekend to come to an end. "I guess that's it." Michelle looks at everyone's empty food containers. "We should probably hit the road. We still have a couple of hours ahead of us."

"I suppose you're right. Unfortunately." Mark bends over to untie Charley.

Justin and Michelle walk toward the truck, and she wraps her arm around him and pulls him toward her, feeling the sadness of their upcoming goodbye.

"Let's go, Charley!" Mark and the happy pup run up behind Michelle and Justin, passing them by, Charley bouncing through the air. Mark opens the truck doors for everyone, and Charley hops in and snuggles in his bed.

Michelle and Justin follow behind, then Marks drives out of the parking lot. It's a quiet ride to Justin's house.

"You can park in front of the garage." Justin points ahead. "Are you guys coming in for a bit?"

"As much as we would love to stay for a while, we'll help you with your things and then we should go. It's a long ride still and we need to get some work done when we get home." Michelle moves her lips into a playful frown.

"Yeah, I get it." Justin grabs his large black duffel bag and walks up the stairs to his front door. "Sushi and Sardine, I'm home," he calls to his cats. They both sit at the top of the stairs looking down at Justin, making it clear they aren't going to put in the effort to walk down.

Charley looks up the stairs at the cats and makes a low, underwhelming growl sound, while he enthusiastically wags his tail.

"Alright, sweetheart, we better go. I love you very much! I'm so happy that you were able to come this weekend. It was an absolute blast. Of course, the time went way too quickly." Michelle hugs Justin tightly as her eyes become blurry with tears. Most of her goodbyes with Justin involve tears.

"I love you, Mom. It was such a great weekend. Thank you for everything. I'll talk to you tomorrow."

Mark and Justin turn to each other and hug. "I love you, buddy. We enjoyed the weekend with you."

"I love you, too. Drive safely. Text me when you guys get home. Goodbye, Charley." Justin bends over and kisses Charley's wet nose.

Mark pulls out of the driveway while everyone is waving goodbye. Michelle wipes her eyes and misses him already.

"Homeward bound."

Mark turns to Michelle and brushes the hair from her face.

Michelle opens her eyes and notices the elementary school that is just a few blocks from their home. "We're home already?"

"We are. Charley said your snoring kept him awake the entire ride."

Michelle laughs. "Well, that's hysterical because I don't snore." She turns back to look at Charley. "Did you say that?"

"Even though it's sad to end a wonderful trip, it's always good to be home." Michelle grabs her bags from the back of the truck, and Mark holds the front door open for her and Charley. "I'm going to get settled and then spend a little time in my office getting caught up on emails since I didn't really check anything this weekend." She leans in to kiss Mark.

"That works. I'll unload the truck and get caught up on work also."

Michelle unpacks her bags and gets a few things settled in the house. She grabs the mail from the kitchen counter, walks down the stairs to her office, flips open her laptop, and looks out the window, watching the woman across the street watering her hydrangeas. She turns back to her computer and starts sorting through her emails, noticing an email from her dad. *That's weird. He usually emails me on Monday afternoons.* The email was sent on Saturday morning.

Good morning, Michelle,

I know you are visiting your aunts this weekend, so I don't expect you to see this until you get back home. I hope you enjoyed your visit.

If you're not sitting down while you're reading this, you may want to. I had a sore by my nose for many years and had it removed last week. It was Basil cancer. They might go in again if any is remaining, but for now it's good and is healing nicely. When I had it removed, I mentioned to the doctor that I had a sore throat for about a week prior, so he looked at that also. The doctor took a sample from my throat and called on Friday to let me know it is cancer. He is going to schedule me for a CT scan to get a better look at it and understand what we're dealing with. We will know more when I go in for the scans. I will keep you updated.

I'm sorry to have to let you know in an email. It's difficult to talk about, so I took the easy way out and emailed you instead of having a phone conversation. I hope you understand. Please don't worry.

Love you,

Dad

Michelle's eyes freeze on the word cancer. *Cancer. Fucking cancer. Oh, Dad, I'm so sorry.* Michelle immediately thinks of her best friend, Colleen, who passed away from breast cancer just over twenty years ago. She recalls how sick Colleen became undergoing radiation and chemo. It was a desperate battle and weeks of complete hell. It sickens Michelle to think of her dad going through that same torture. She feels helpless and wishes she could make it go away for him. Her insides fill with fury as she thinks of all the times as a child her mom wished her dad dead. 'I can't wait to piss on his grave' her mom would say. *My god, she's a monster.* Michelle can feel her cheeks wetten from the tears streaming down her face. She turns toward her office doorway, and Mark is leaning against the wall with concern in his eyes.

"What's the matter, honey?" He walks toward her and gently kisses her head.

Michelle looks up at Mark with her tearful eyes, struggles to find her voice, and painfully mutters the words, "My dad has throat cancer."

CHAPTER TWELVE

SESSION FOUR

The glare from the late August sun is burning Michelle's eyes. She puts down the sun visor in her car, but the rays continue to beat on her face. *Why didn't I grab my sunglasses from my other purse?* She carefully navigates between the glares bouncing off other cars and pulls into the always full parking lot of her therapist's office. Despite the challenge of driving in the sun without her sunglasses, Michelle fully embraces its presence and the warm weather. Especially this time of year. She gets giddy just thinking about the end of summer, which means her favorite season is crawling around the corner. Autumn. The way the sun hits the leaves on the trees turning brilliant shades of red, yellow, and orange. The crispness in the air that makes you excited to grab a sweatshirt before stepping outside. The constant smell in the air of bonfires. Michelle shakes her head and stops daydreaming about the most beautiful season ever. *Dr. Tyson, I have a lot for you today.* Michelle shuts the car door behind her and briskly walks through the parking lot.

She approaches the front desk, and there is a young man sitting in the seat she usually waits in. "Hi, Renee, I'm here for my one o'clock appointment with Dr. Tyson."

"Hi, Michelle, I'll let her know you're here. Feel free to have a seat." Renee smiles at Michelle and nods toward the available chairs.

Michelle sits down in the chair next to the front door and unknowingly glances at the gentleman waiting. They make eye contact, briefly smile, and turn away. She grabs her phone and swipes up to turn on the Do Not Disturb setting.

"Mr. Davis?" A dark haired, very tall, and slightly intimidating man smiles, looking at the young man waiting. They shake hands and he follows him down the hallway. Michelle tries not to watch but she's always intrigued by other people's personal lives. *I wonder what he has going on in his life that he needs to talk to a therapist about. Maybe I should have been a therapist, then I would get to hear people's deep dark secrets.*

Michelle and Mark often study people when they're in public and create their own scenarios for what a particular stranger does for a living, how they met the person they're standing next to, some drama that they have in their life. It's become a common form of entertainment for them both.

"Hi, Michelle, I'm ready for you." Dr. Tyson greets Michelle with her usual kind and genuine smile.

"Hi Dr. Tyson." Michelle smiles back and follows her to her office. When she walks in, her eyes widen in delight.

"I redecorated." Dr. Tyson smirks at Michelle. "I was getting the fall bug so bought some new pillows and changed some other things out to bring in the warmth of autumn. What do you think?"

"I absolutely love it. Everything looks great!" Michelle grins widely and feels a deeper level of comfort each time they meet. She walks over to the white couch that is now covered in deep orange and golden yellow throw pillows. They conveniently complement the clear glass vase on the coffee table filled with an assortment of orange, red, and yellow artificial flowers. The room looks like a display from the Pottery Barn. There is a cream-colored chunky blanket draped over the arm of the couch, and although it's eighty-two degrees outside and Michelle is wearing a short sleeve blouse and denim skirt, she still opts for the blanket. This will be a new source of comfort for her. She moves the pillows out of the way, sits on the couch, and pulls the blanket across her lap, folding over a portion for her hands to twist.

"How have you been since our last visit?" Dr. Tyson sits in her chair and takes a sip from her pink, floral, coffee mug.

Michelle briefly replays in her head everything that has happened over the last couple of weeks. They had to reschedule last week's session due to Dr. Tyson planning some last-minute time off to spend with her two kids and get them ready for school before the new school year begins.

"I'm doing okay. There has been an overwhelming number of things since I saw you last."

Dr. Tyson raises an eyebrow. "Alright. Good things?"

Michelle sits back in the couch, pulling the blanket closer to her stomach. "Some good, but mostly not. I'll start with the positive. Mark, Justin, and I visited my aunts and their families last weekend. It was so long overdue, and I was filled with such gratitude all weekend. While I'm sad for the years lost, I remind myself to be thankful for where I'm at now. It took most of my life to figure out who I can trust and who truly is there for me. While it's a shame it took so long, I guess I'll use the old cliché, 'better late than never'."

"You are absolutely correct, Michelle." She kindly smiles, looking proud of Michelle's progress. "I'm happy to hear that you're showing gratitude for what you've overcome and where you are now rather than focusing on the negative path it took you to get here. Tell me about the not so good things that you are referring to."

Michelle contemplates what she should begin with. "I obtained my parent's divorce case. I think I mentioned in a previous session that I wanted to know why they got divorced. After recently learning about all the mistruths that Mom and Kevin had fed me, and her siblings, something in my gut was telling me I needed to find out what happened with my mom and dad."

Dr. Tyson looks at Michelle intently, holding the pen in her notebook. "Did you find anything surprising?'

'You could say that.' Michelle twists the blanket between her hands, still appalled by the revelation. "My mom left me and my dad to be with Kevin. My dad filed for divorce because she left us for another man." Michelle can hear the quavering in her voice. "They always told me that Mom filed for divorce because Dad didn't treat her well and that Kevin waited years before dating my mom."

"How did you feel when you saw this information in the divorce case?" Dr. Tyson continues writing and doesn't look up from her notebook.

Michelle gives an exasperated sigh. "I was overcome with what felt like hundreds of emotions at once. Shock, disgust, anger, confusion, betrayal, to name a few. I couldn't believe what I was reading."

Dr. Tyson nods. "Those emotions all make sense. I'm sure it was hard to process what you were reading. You grew up believing in an entirely different story. Did you find anything else unexpected in the case?"

"Yes, my dad tried his damndest to get custody of me. In fact, the Guardian ad Litem said he would be the better choice.

But after home visits and psychological evaluations, the court awarded Mom custody. There wasn't any indication or passion on her behalf that showed she wanted custody. I think my grandparents encouraged her, telling her it was the right thing to do. It wasn't what she wanted. During the home visits, when she was asked why she should have custody, her response was because we were both female and can relate to each other, and she provides food and clothing." Michelle shakes her head.

"Those are pretty basic reasons to justify getting custody. You mentioned your dad put a lot more effort into getting custody of you. What did he do?"

"Well, he received his master's degree in counselor education, so his background consisted of psychology and sociology. He had plans to have me participate in church and school activities as well as girl scouts. He had visitation rights during the custody battle, and he referred to us going for bike rides, picnics, and trips to the library. In fact, he worked as a house parent for eighteen girls so he would have a better idea of things I would face as a girl growing up. The Guardian ad Litem noted that Dad had pictures of me all over his house and Dad would get excited talking about our upcoming weekends together." She could envision her dad having those conversations. "Dad sincerely and genuinely wanted to raise me. And most importantly, nowhere in that case was there any mention of my dad sexually assaulting me or harming me in anyway."

Dr. Tyson stops writing and looks up. "How do you react to that?"

Michelle inhales deeply and looks out the window. "I feel a lot of things about that. Relief. I'm beyond grateful that it never happened to me. Sadness. My relationship with my dad ended when I was told that. Hatred. That my mom told me an unforgivable lie that negatively impacted my life in so many ways. Honestly, reading the divorce case gave me closure on the relationship with my mother. It validated that she and Kevin are truly horrible human beings, and I lost any respect that I ever had for either of them. I can sincerely say that they are nothing to me now."

"That's understandable, and having closure is a good place to be. You've uncovered a great deal of information that is life altering." Dr. Tyson looks at Michelle reassuringly. "Now that you have closure, what does that mean to you?"

"It means that I can stop blaming myself for not having a relationship with my mother. I did nothing wrong. I'm not a bad person, and I wasn't a bad daughter. I was a great daughter, and I need to remember that. It means that I can move forward and never look back, wondering if I did something different then maybe she would have been approving of me or wanted to be a part of my life. It means that I know the truth now, and I'm thankful for that." Michelle rubs her arm in an effort to comfort herself.

"Please keep telling yourself all those things. You are not a bad person; and you did nothing to deserve the treatment you received from your mother. You know, Michelle, this is our fourth session together and it amazes me to see the work that you've put in to get yourself into a better place. You've had a lot to overcome, not only your entire life but recently as well. You should be very proud of yourself. It doesn't happen overnight, and some days it may be more difficult. Some weeks or months may be more difficult, but if you keep working on taking care of yourself, knowing what you deserve and continue using the techniques from your toolbox you will continue to be in a desired state of mind. With that being said, I think we can schedule our sessions every two weeks instead of weekly. And yes, you are right. A lot has happened since our last session. Was there anything else?"

Michelle looks down at her lap. "Yes, unfortunately, there is one more thing." She stops for a minute to find the strength to utter the horrible words. "I found out last week that my dad has throat cancer."

"Oh, Michelle, I'm so sorry."

"Yeah, the one parent who cares for me and loves me has cancer." She pauses and fights back the tears that are ready to pour out. "He was a cigarette smoker pretty much his entire life. It's just so devastating. I asked him if we could come and visit but he said we should hold off on the visits for now. I understand that. He's going to be going through a lot. I just feel helpless. I know it's not about me at all, but I want to be there for him. It's sad to say, but we don't have a typical father-daughter relationship due to the twenty-five years we lost and the damage that's been done. We lost so much. I knew him the best when I was a little girl." She will forever be devastated by the years that were lost. "We reestablished our relationship later in life, and that is wonderful, but we missed out on so much of each other's lives and who we really are. I understand that it's probably difficult for him to ask me for help or expect me to be there for him, and that breaks my heart. I want to assist in taking him to treatments if that's helpful. I want to do anything I possibly can to help him get through this. I will continue to offer, check in on him, and pray for him to have the strength and will to get through this. If I can do more, I will. He goes for his scans next week, so we'll know more then."

"I imagine your dad is going through a lot right now. Just processing the fact that he has cancer is frightening and overwhelming. It sounds like you and your dad are in such a good place now, after all these years, and I'm confident that he knows that you are there for him. And honestly, that could be the very best thing he needs. Keep doing what you're doing."

Dr. Tyson's timer chimes. "Michelle, this was a great session, and you shared a lot today. Please take care of yourself and continue working on the meditation techniques. Can I give you a hug?"

Michelle's eyes fill with tears, and she leans in to embrace Dr. Tyson. She can't stop the tears at this point. It's two weeks' worth of emotions running down her face.

"I'm sorry." Michelle pulls away and wipes her eyes.

"Remember, we don't apologize for tears. Crying is healthy and will help ease your emotional pain." Dr. Tyson holds out the Kleenex box.

"Thank you." Michelle takes a couple of tissues and wipes the tears.

Dr. Tyson walks her to the doorway and rubs Michelle's arm. "I'll see you in two weeks then."

"See you then. Thank you, Dr. Tyson." Michelle walks down the hallway toward the front door, looking down, not wanting to draw attention to her red puffy eyes. *Of course, there are two people in the waiting room. There is never anyone in the waiting room.* Michelle notices Renee is away from her desk. *Thank goodness.*

She walks out of the building and stops at the curb, scanning the parking lot. *Where did I park?*

She spots her car two rows over, parked tightly in between a white pick-up truck and red minivan.

She squeezes in the driver's side, leans her head back on the head rest, and feels numb all over. *Therapy is exhausting.*

CHAPTER THIRTEEN

THE GLOW

Michelle walks over to the kitchen counter and picks up her phone. She looks at the screen, squinting her eyes. "It's just one of those motion detected notifications for Mom and Kevin's security cameras."

"I can't believe they never removed your access to their security system." Mark clears the dishes from the kitchen table.

"Kevin probably forgot that he even had me set up with access. It was years ago when they first got the security system, and they were just testing it out." The phone continues to buzz. Michelle typically doesn't look at the notifications, as they're more of an annoyance than anything. Occasionally she'll look to be nosey, but there's never anything worth looking at. It's usually an animal, their guests, or her mom or Kevin setting off the cameras, and she has no interest in any of those things anymore. Michelle clicks into the alert and sees an image of a man walking along a line of pine trees behind the lodge. She takes her thumb and first finger and makes the image larger. "No way. That can't be him. Wow, Kevin is a frail old man."

Michelle hands her phone to Mark. He takes the phone, focusing in on the image. His eyes widen. "That's Kevin?" He continues to study the man on Michelle's phone. "I guess it is him. He looks like he's ninety pounds and a hundred years old. Now that the lodge is off the market, I'm guessing that's where they'll be spending their retirement years and the rest of their lives. It doesn't look like it's boding well for him."

"Out of curiosity I want to go into the security app and see if I can see Mom." She holds out her hand for the phone. Michelle scrolls her finger across the screen and finds the app, taps the phone, and selects the camera that just set off the notification. "There she is." Michelle feels her hands start shaking and her heart pounding through her chest. She hasn't seen her mom in over a year and a half. The sight of her makes her nauseous. "She looks even more feeble than Kevin. She was always too thin anyway, now she's just a bag of bones." Michelle takes her two fingers and zooms in on her mom holding a large orange bucket, throwing feed for the chickens. "Do you want to take a look?"

Mark takes the phone and stares at the screen. "You would have thought it's been fifteen years since we've seen them last. Lonely and miserable isn't a good look for them."

"I've seen enough. You can put the phone down when you're done looking."

Mark sets the phone back on the kitchen counter, turns toward Michelle, and pulls her in for a hug. "Are you okay?"

She rests her head on his chest. "I guess. It's like watching ghosts from a different lifetime. Maybe I should just get rid of that app. It would be nice to not have the annoying notifications lighting up my phone. And I don't need any reminder of them in my life anymore. I just thought it would be good to keep and have access so I could have the ability to be nosey when I wanted to. But after seeing them, I think I'm good without."

"I understand. Well think about it. You don't have to do anything with it now." Mark gives her a kiss on the cheek and turns to grab his wine glass from the table.

"You're right. I don't have to worry about it right now." Michelle immerses her hands into the soapy dishwater and tries to erase the images of her mom and Kevin. Seeing them on the security camera stirs up her anxiety and all the bad memories that she's trying to move forward from. *How can such a timid soul be such a horrible monster?*

"What time are you waking up tomorrow?" She dries her hands and neatly folds the towel on the counter.

"I don't even want to talk about that." Mark throws his head back on the couch. "It's going to be a rough one. I set the alarm for two a.m. and will leave by two-thirty. It's an hour to the airport and my flight is at five, so that should be plenty of time. I wish Charley's dog sitter was available so you could join me."

"I wish I could go too. You need to be there though for the start of the project, so we don't have a lot of flexibility regarding timing. Charley and I will be just fine." Michelle kneels on the floor, rubbing Charley's belly. "Isn't that right, Charley." She turns to look at Mark. "Should we call it a night since it's going to be an early one?"

"Yes, I suppose." Mark gets up from the couch. "Alright, Charley, let's go outside."

Michelle stares into the vanity mirror hanging over the bathroom sink, watching her reflection mindlessly as she brushes her teeth. She rinses her mouth, swishing vigorously, and spits into the sink. As she wipes her mouth, this time she intently looks at her reflection, staring at her tired face, noticing the lines around her eyes, showing her age. Her hair flops on her head in a messy bun. She looks deep into her blue eyes, grins, and tells herself *I love you*. Those three words have been easier to tell herself lately, since she has had the courage and strength to separate herself from her relationship with her mother. Each day she feels stronger, happier, and in a much better place.

She switches off the bathroom light and walks down the hallway to their bedroom. She turns on the lamp on her nightstand and taps her phone to see what time it is. Her screen is filled with motion detected notifications. She slowly sits on the bed, not taking her eyes off the phone and scrolls through the alerts. *There must be over thirty notifications. I've never seen so many. The alerts are coming from all ten security cameras at Mom and Kevin's lodge.* Michelle raises her legs to the bed and crosses them underneath her. *What is that orange glare? It's nine at night.* She taps her phone and opens one of the alerts. All she sees is a bright glow. She clicks open another notification. The same bright glow. She scrolls to the security app and touches the first camera option she sees. Michelle's jaw drops open and her eyes become wide with fear. *Oh my god! OH MY GOD! There are flames everywhere!* Michelle gasps frantically. *What do I do? Do I call 911? What the hell happened?* She quickly clicks on another security camera in the app. Black. That camera is down. She opens the next camera. Flames fill the entire screen of her phone. She can't make out any part of the buildings. She's filled with panic, clicking into each of the camera settings. Most views are just black at this point. Only half of the cameras are working, she remembers they had a few cameras attached to tree tops and light poles, those cameras must still be intact. Her heart sinks. *I can't believe this is happening. I hope everyone is okay. All the animals. The poor animals. What if they had guests? Oh my god, this is terrifying.*

Michelle tries to hold her shaking hands still and presses 9-1-1.

"Nine-one-one. What's your emergency?"

"I want to report a fire at 4852 County Road 24." Michelle can't get the words out fast enough. "It's just South of Omaha, it's The Back 40 Lodge. There are flames everywhere."

"Thank you, ma'am. 4852 County Road 24." Michelle can hear the gentleman typing away as he repeats the information. "This has already been reported and crews are on their way to the scene."

"Oh, thank God. Thank you so much." Michelle feels a brief moment of relief.

"Mark, you need to come here!" Michelle doesn't move and continues to make her way through each of the camera views.

The cameras that are still working show a fiery scene completely out of control. *Everything is burning!* She looks closely to see if she can see any people or any of their animals, but the only thing she sees are flames dancing uncontrollably while black smoke billows into the sky. Michelle desperately switches from one camera to the next, trying to understand what she's looking at. She starts to make out parts of the main lodge and notices the wraparound porch swallowed in the blaze. She opens another camera and sees four silhouettes crawling on the ground through plumes of smoke. She zooms in closer but can't identify any details of the four people fighting for their lives. She holds the phone to her ear and can hear the faint sound of sirens. *They're almost there.* Michelle exhales and continues switching from camera to camera. The sirens are screaming, lights are beaming. *Three firetrucks?* She watches as several firefighters pour out of their trucks and start hosing down the flames surrounding them.

"What's going on?" Mark stands in the doorway and looks at Michelle with confusion.

"You'll never believe this. The lodge is on fire! The flames are everywhere! Everything is burning." She holds out her phone.

Mark leans in closer, and his eyes grow huge in disbelief. "Holy shit! How in the world did that happen?"

Michelle nods with fear and dismay in her eyes. "I came out of the bathroom and my phone was filled with alerts. I looked and just saw this bright glow and then realized their entire property was on fire. I can't even believe it. I'm in shock."

"It's horrifying! How could that even happen? And to get so out of control. Oh my god. I hope everyone is okay and got out of the lodge before the fire engulfed the entire building." Marks sits on the bed next to Michelle as they watch the firefighters continue to battle the blaze.

"I'm going to call Linda." She scrolls out of the security app and taps Linda's contact info. "I didn't even look at the time. It's ten? Dammit, I'll be waking them up." Michelle looks at Mark while the phone is ringing.

"Michelle? Is everything okay?" Linda answers the phone groggily.

"Linda, I'm so sorry to wake you. Mom and Kevin's lodge is on fire. It's destroying pretty much everything. Fire crews are there now." Michelle's voice is trembling.

"What? You have got to be kidding me!" Linda is suddenly wide awake.

"I was getting all the motion detected alerts on my phone from their security network and saw the fire. Linda, it's horrible."

"I'm in complete shock. Joe's up now. We'll drive over and see if we can find anything out and make sure everyone is okay. Thank you for letting us know." Michelle can sense the distress in Linda's voice.

"Please be careful and let me know what you find out."

"We will. I'll talk to you soon."

Michelle looks at Mark in disbelief. He rubs her back as she rests her head on his shoulder.

She goes back into her phone, the flames have slightly diminished, but the black smoke fills the night sky. Michelle and Mark continue viewing the different security cameras, trying to find some sign of life. "Oh no! That was the loafing shed." Michelle holds her hand to her mouth. "The horses." Michelle watches a firefighter hosing down the flames that destroyed what was once the shed that housed the horses. "It's just a pile of charred wood. There is no way the horses survived that." Michelle's heart sinks.

They continue watching the destruction in awe, acknowledging that the whole thing is just a terrifying nightmare that they won't be waking up from.

"Mark, it's eleven. You're not going to get any sleep."

"I couldn't sleep now if I wanted to. We need to keep our eye on this."

Michelle's phone rings and she quickly answers it. "Hi Linda."

"We can't get anywhere close to the property. They have the road closed. We can see all the smoke though. It's billowing for miles. An ambulance passed us on the way, I'm guessing they were headed to the lodge."

"Wow, this is just so unbelievable. I don't even know what to do. Are you going back home now?"

"Yes, we're headed back now. I won't be able to sleep tonight, so if you need anything, please call."

"Okay, be safe. Text when you get home." Michelle ends the call and clicks back into the security cameras. At this point, cameras four, eight, and ten are the only working cameras.

"I'm not seeing an ambulance from any of these views."

"These are the cameras for the back and side of the lodge." Mark points at Michelle's phone.

The entire night, they continue switching between the three camera views, watching as the firefighters put out the remaining flames. "What is that? Over by the lake?" Michelle points at the image.

They both lean in closer, trying to identify what looks like a large spot hidden in clouds of smoke.

"I think that it might be one of their horses." Mark says with uncertainty.

"My goodness, I think you're right." Michelle feels slightly comforted.

Mark's phone starts chiming, and they look at each other immediately.

"You're alarm! Oh no. Mark, I'm so sorry. You're going to be exhausted."

"It's all good. I'll sleep on the plane. I'm still wired anyway."

"Please be careful getting to the airport."

"I will. I'll let you know when I get there. You should try to get some sleep."

She crawls under the covers still watching her phone, hoping to see more signs of life.

Michelle awakes to the sun on her face, her phone in her hand. She opens her eyes and immediately thinks of the fire. She opens one of the security cameras, and the daylight is shedding a new perspective. The grounds are covered in ashes, burnt wood and personal belongings. She scans the property and there isn't one standing building. She focuses in on the main lodge. Part of the structure is still standing, but it's surrounded by massive piles of charred wood and remnants of furniture. She zooms in closer and can see a bed frame and bathroom sink. She switches cameras and spots where the loafing shed used to be. It's a heap of rubble still smoldering. *It looks like a war zone. The entire property is completely lifeless. What happened to all the animals? Did Mom and Kevin survive? And their guests? How did the fire even start?* Michelle is appalled by all of it.

She rolls out of bed and throws on her robe. *Let's go downstairs, Charley.*

Michelle sits at her desk and opens her computer. She opens a browser and searches *Fire at The Back 40 Lodge.* Images appear immediately. The pictures are comparable to what she was watching last night. She clicks on the link for the first article available.

Emergency crews responded to a fire late Sunday evening at The Back 40 Lodge, located 20 miles South of Omaha, Nebraska. The massive fire destroyed several buildings, including the main lodge and a loafing shed that housed the owner's animals. Officials say two people were found dead and 3 are being hospitalized for smoke inhalation. No identities have been shared at this time. More than 4 horses, 2 dogs, 6 cats, and several chickens also died in the fire. The cause of the fire is currently under investigation. This is an ongoing story and will be updated when more information becomes available.

Michelle falls back in her chair and looks away from the computer. *Oh dear god! Two people are dead? Mom? Kevin? Guests? Who died? My god, I need to find out who died!* She picks up her phone and scrolls through her contact list. Her finger clicking on *Mom.* Michelle stares out the window, becoming more anxious with each unanswered ring. After four rings, she is sent to voicemail. Michelle is feeling panicked.

"Mom, it's Michelle. I heard about the fire last night. Are you okay? This is absolutely terrifying. I don't even know what to say. I just wanted to call and make sure you and Kevin are safe. Please call back." Michelle finds herself stuttering the words as she can't form the sentences fast enough.

Why isn't she answering? Her mind is spinning even more, wondering why her mom's phone went unanswered. Michelle scrolls through the contacts again and taps her finger on *Kevin. Oh my god, somebody pick up, please.* Michelle paces her office, looking at the floor. *Fuck, voicemail.* She slams her phone on her desk and continues pacing. *This is horrible. No one is answering. My god, are they both dead?* She picks up her phone again and searches for the number for the Sheriff's Office.

"Douglas County Sheriff's Office, how may I help you," answers a woman with a kind and calming voice.

"Hi, my name is Michelle Dupree." Her voice is trembling. "My parents own The Back 40 Lodge. I understand there was a fire last night that destroyed the property and left two people deceased. I can't reach my parents and I was hoping that you could help me."

"Sure, ma'am. One second please, I'll transfer you to the Sheriff."

"Thank you so much," Michelle replied, reminding herself to keep breathing.

"Sheriff Carter," A deep, gruff voice answers.

"Yes, hello, Sheriff. My name is Michelle Dupree. I was explaining to the woman that my parents own The Back 40 Lodge and I'm unable to reach them. I know about the fire last night. I want to be sure that they are safe and unharmed. Are you able to provide me with any information? I'm not sure who else to call right now."

"I'm more than happy to assist you, Ms. Dupree. First off, my sincere condolences for this tragedy. It's devastating. We are all in disbelief. One second, please, while I grab the paperwork from the Medical Examiner."

"Thank you, Sheriff." Michelle leans forward in her chair, trying to prepare herself for what she is about to learn.

"Alright, Ms. Dupree, I have the forms from the Medical Examiner. The names of the deceased are Kevin Meyer and Dan Weber. It sounds like the three that were hospitalized will be just fine and released later today from Methodist Hospital."

Michelle is in shock. "Oh god. Kevin is my stepfather. The other gentleman must have been a guest at the lodge. Was Mary Meyer one of the people hospitalized? She's my mother."

"Yes, ma'am. The latest update I received advised that she will be just fine and released this afternoon. Is there anything else that I can help you with?"

"Thank you. No, you've been extremely helpful. I greatly appreciate it."

"You're more than welcome. Again, my sincere condolences, I'm so sorry for your loss. Please call if I can be of further assistance."

"Thank you, Sheriff." Michelle ends the call. *Kevin is dead. Oh my god. I can't even wrap my head around this. The only two things that meant anything to my mom, the lodge and Kevin, and now they're both gone. I need to call Linda.*

"Hi Michelle. I imagine you didn't get any sleep last night."

"Hi, Linda. I didn't. This whole thing is just unbelievable. Early this morning I found an article regarding the fire, and it stated that two people were found dead and three were sent to the hospital for smoke inhalation. I tried calling Mom right away and she didn't answer. Then I tried Kevin, he didn't answer, either. So, I called the Sheriff."

"Two people are dead? What did the sheriff say?"

"You probably want to sit down for this." Michelle's voice cracks as she speaks. "Kevin is dead."

"What? Oh my god! He's dead? And your mom?"

"Mom went to the hospital for smoke inhalation, she'll be fine and released this afternoon. I didn't recognize the name of the other person who died, so he must have been a guest."

"Oh, Michelle, this is horrible. Are you okay?" Linda asked, her voice full of concern.

"I'm in shock right now. I don't even know what to do."

"Yes, this is extremely tragic. I completely understand. I'll let Joe and everyone else know. Please call me if there is anything at all that you need and when you find out more information."

"I will, thank you, Linda. I love you."

"I love you, too."

Michelle sits numbly, staring out the window feeling helpless and exhausted with grief and anguish. *How did this happen? What is Mom going to do?*

With her phone still in her hand, she searches Methodist Hospital and clicks the call icon. After two rings, she's connected to the phone tree and presses three for the nurse's station.

"Good morning, Methodist Hospital, this is Amy, how may I help you?"

"Hi, Amy, I'm trying to reach a patient who was admitted last night. Her name is Mary Meyer. I'm her daughter."

"One second please, let me check the system to see if we have anyone by that name," the overly cheerful woman replied.

"Here we are. Yes, it looks like Mary Meyer was admitted last night. Would you like me to transfer you to her room?"

"Yes, please. Thank you so much." Michelle breathes a sigh of relief in locating her mother.

"You're very welcome. One moment."

Michelle anxiously taps her finger on her desk as the phone rings. After the fourth ring and no answer, Michelle hangs up, frustrated. She scrolls down the recent call history and clicks on *Mom*; the call goes directly to voicemail.

"Mom, it's Michelle again. I spoke with the Sheriff. I'm so sorry to hear about Kevin. I know you're in the hospital and will be released today. I tried calling your room, but no one answered. I'm glad to know that you will be okay. I can't even imagine what you're going through. I'm here for you if you need anything at all." Michelle ends the call, holds the phone to her chest, and sits in silence.

CHAPTER FOURTEEN

FIFTY-ONE

Michelle's eyes open to Charley kissing her face. "Good morning, Charley. Thank you for the love." She rolls over and Mark's side of the bed is empty. *Something smells delicious.* She turns back over and notices the time. *Ten o'clock? I never sleep in.* She throws the covers off and follows the inviting aroma.

"What is all this?" Michelle beams with excitement. The kitchen table is covered with a bouquet of wildflowers, cheese omelets, fresh strawberries, cinnamon rolls, coffee, and cranberry mimosas.

"Happy birthday, sweetheart!" Mark leans in for a birthday kiss. He grabs the two glasses of mimosas, and they clink them cheerfully.

"Thank you so much! Honey, you are the best. What did I do to deserve you?" Michelle pulls out the chair. "It all looks so tasty. Now I'm starving. I didn't even hear you get out of bed."

"I was trying my best not to wake you. I wanted you to sleep in." Mark sits at the table and spoons some strawberries onto his plate.

"Mark, this is scrumptious. What a fun birthday surprise! That was very sweet and thoughtful of you. Thank you."

"You're very welcome. You deserve it. It's crazy to think that a year ago we were in San Diego."

"I know, that was such a great trip. It's hard to believe it's been a year already. This year has been monumental for sure. There is definitely a lot to celebrate." Michelle grins widely and holds up her mimosa. "I'm really looking forward to dinner tonight. It's going to be wonderful to see everyone."

"Reservations are for six, right?"

"Yes, six. Everyone is meeting at the restaurant. We have a room reserved since we're expecting twenty-five people."

"Perfect. That is so great that everyone can make it. Can I get you anything else to eat?" Mark grabs another cinnamon roll.

"No, but I'll take another mimosa." She winks at Mark.

"Coming right up." Mark pours two more mimosas and hands one to Michelle. "I'll take care of cleaning everything up. Enjoy your mimosa outside if you want."

"Yes, that is a lovely idea. Seriously, thank you so much for all of this. It was perfect." She smiles glowingly and kisses Mark on the cheek. "I'll be on the deck enjoying my mimosa with the sun on my face."

"Enjoy, birthday girl!" Mark clears the plates from the table.

Michelle closes the patio door behind her and curls up on the loveseat. She sips her mimosa and savors the bubbles dancing on her tongue, breathing in the fresh spring air, grateful for this moment. She soaks in every single second and appreciates the view of the tulips starting to bloom, the robins bouncing on the budding branches, and the neighbor kids playing catch in their muddy yard. Spring always offers a sense of newness and fresh starts. Michelle reflects on the past year and feels a sense of pride in how much she has overcome and how she made self-love a priority. Although Michelle has worked diligently to get herself into a better place mentally and emotionally, the year has definitely been a roller coaster of events and emotions. Reuniting with her aunts was certainly a highlight of the year. She received the wonderful news that her dad is in remission. Therapy has been constructive, especially from the sense of knowing that it's okay to let go of unhealthy relationships. Then there was the fire that took Kevin's life and destroyed their property. Clearly this was the low point of the year. Though Michelle continued to struggle with her relationship with her mother, she had set all of that aside and reached out to her mom continuously after the fire. Michelle found the strength to move forward and no longer hold on to the negativity and resentment of her past. All of the calls she made to her mother remain unreturned.

Michelle's phone buzzes. She grabs it and sees Justin's face. "Good morning, Justin, how are you?"

"Happy birthday to you! Happy birthday to you! Happy Birthday, dear Mom, happy birthday to you!" Michelle warmly smiles as Justin sings her birthday greeting. "Happy birthday, Mom. How's your day so far?"

"Aww, thank you for that. My birthday is off to a great start. I slept in, and Mark made breakfast for me, which was so delicious. Now I'm enjoying a mimosa on the deck and talking to my favorite son."

"That's what I like to hear. It sounds like the perfect start to your birthday, Mom. I'm looking forward to seeing you guys this evening and celebrating your day. Who's all coming?"

"Me too. I'm beyond excited for tonight. There will be twenty-five of us, so we have a room reserved. It will be all my aunts and their families, your grandpa, and Lori. It means the world to me that everyone is coming."

"That is so awesome. It will be so good to see everyone, especially Grandpa. I haven't seen him since we found out he's in remission."

"I know, it's pretty remarkable." Michelle beams as she stares into the blue sky. "We'll meet you there at six then?"

"That works, I'll see you then. Happy birthday, Mom. I love you so much!"

"I love you, Justin. Thank you for the birthday song. See you tonight!" Michelle sets the phone on the ottoman.

She sips the last of her mimosa and grabs her phone again. *I haven't looked at the security cameras at the lodge for several months now.* She stopped checking on the cameras a few months ago, shortly after the fire. Michelle went to the property many times after the fire in hopes of finding her mom, since she wasn't reaching her by phone. Every time she went, it was lonely, barren, with no signs of life.

Michelle clicks the app and opens camera four. She narrows her eyes and scans the view. *Wow, it's so desolate.* She sees the charred foundation filled with burnt wood slabs and piles of ashes. She opens camera eight, the view of the far side of what used to be the lodge. *That's new. A shed?* She zooms in on the new structure that's tucked in the trees that were untouched by the fire. *Is someone living in there?* She notices a light shining behind white curtains but can't make out anything through the covered windows. She clicks into camera ten. The view along the line of pine trees. *Oh my god, is that a person?* She sees a silhouette shadowed by the towering pines and adjusts the image on her phone. *There are way too many shadows.* She intently stares at her phone but can't identify any characteristics. The figure moves further back into the pine trees. *No way, it can't be.* Michelle focuses on a second shape. *It sure is. Junior.* The German Shepard her mom and Kevin got after Duke passed away several years ago. *Junior survived.* She watches closely. *They're walking too far into the trees now. Aww, Junior, you're limping. You got lucky, I guess.* Michelle puts the phone in her lap, trying to piece together what she had just seen. *Mom must be living in that shed with Junior.* A part of Michelle feels grateful to know where her mom is, but a larger part is heart wrenching. *Wow. She must really hate me to never have returned my calls or accept my offers for help.* Michelle stares into the yard. *She would rather be alone than have me in her life.*

Michelle's attention is diverted by the barking of the neighbor's dogs. She grabs her empty glass and phone and walks back inside.

~ ~ ~

Mark walks around the car and opens Michelle's door. "Here we are. Are you ready?"

"I'm so ready." Michelle takes Mark's hand as she gets out of the car. They walk under the ivy pergola and through the front door as he holds it open, following her inside.

Eno Vino is Michelle's favorite restaurant. She and Mark have celebrated many occasions here, including him proposing. The atmosphere always takes her to Italy, even if it's only for a couple of hours until she realizes she's still in Nebraska. All the tables are filled, as usual. They are packed three-deep at the bar, and the restaurant is buzzing with chatter.

"Our room is to the right of the bar." They weave in between the waitstaff and pass the bar.

Michelle stops and stands in the doorway, staring into the room; it's filled with her loved ones standing around talking and laughing. Balloons are tied in bunches and fill each of the corners in the room. A *Happy Birthday, Michelle!* sign in pink and gold hangs from the ceiling. She remains still and watches. Her heart is full. *Everyone is here for me.* She becomes overwhelmed with tears of joy and does her best to hold them back, she doesn't want to ruin her makeup. As much as she can't wait to walk into the room, she holds this moment forever in her mind. Then she turns to Mark with the widest smile and eyes glistening with happy tears. "Let's get this party started." Mark laughs and they continue into the room.

Justin notices them walking toward the group and shouts "Happy birthday!" Everyone else chimes in. Michelle makes her way around the room, exchanging hugs and toasting glasses. The conversations are never ending, and laughter is bouncing off the walls. She turns toward the doorway and notices a short, stalky gentleman in black slacks and a white dress shirt. He appears awkward and seems unsure of who to address. Michelle walks over, "Hi, I'm Michelle."

"Hi, Michelle. I'm Shane, I'll be taking care of your group this evening."

"Nice to meet you, Shane. Thank you so much. Would you like us to take a seat at the table and start ordering?"

"That would be great, the menus are on the table. I'll be back in a few minutes."

"Hey, everyone, that was Shane, and he'll be taking care of us tonight. He'll be coming back in a few minutes to take our orders, so feel free to have a seat and look at the menus."

Michelle finds a spot at the table and sets her drink down. She briskly walks toward the doorway and passes Mark on her way. "I'm going to the restroom quick," she whispers in passing.

She contentedly walks into the main restaurant, it's even busier than when they first arrived. Michelle looks across the bar in the direction of the restroom and squeezes by a group of four men waiting to place their drink order. As she passes the bar making her way to the bathroom, her eyes are drawn to some commotion at the end of the bar. An older frail woman with wiry reddish-gray hair stumbles toward her barstool, bumping into a server, who nearly spills her tray of drinks. The woman pulls herself onto the stool and continues drinking.

Not paying any mind to what just happened. She gets a better look at the woman, and Michelle can't move her feet. Her stomach drops. *You have got to be kidding me. It's her. Just like in my dreams.* Michelle's first reaction is to pretend she didn't see her mother; however, she had a tendency for taking the high road, even at times when she prefers not to. Michelle apprehensively proceeds toward her mom. As she approaches the incapacitated woman, she is in awe by the difference in her appearance. The green dress hangs off her like a bad set of drapes, her skin is almost iridescent, showing all her veins, and her hair is unkempt, as if she just rolled out of bed.

"Mom?" Michelle stands next to the barstool with her arms folded across her chest. Her mother turns toward her with sunken eyes and immediately turns back to face the bar. She slams her empty gin and tonic glass down and the squeezed lime wedge flops on its side.

"I called you day after day after the fire. I'm so sorry to hear about everything. I'm sorry to hear about Kevin. You never returned my calls. We wanted to help. How come you never called me back?' Michelle continues to talk to the side of her mother's face.

"It sounds like you're trying to pick a fight with me, Michelle." Her mother slurs the words, still staring in front of her, now raising her empty glass and shaking it toward the bartender.

"I'm definitely not trying to pick a fight with you. I saw you and wanted to come over and say hi and see how you are." Her mom continues to stare forward, not acknowledging Michelle's presence. "Okay, Mom. I'll leave you be then. Please call if you ever need anything."

Michelle turns away and feels her eyes well up with tears. She makes it into the restroom and shuts the stall door behind her. *Well, some things never change.* She pulls off several squares of toilet paper and dabs her eyes in hopes of preventing a major downpour of tears. *She's not going to get to me today. I have been doing so well, accepting that she will no longer be a part of my life.* Michelle inhales deeply and releases her breath. She opens the stall door and steps toward the sink, staring into the eyes of the fifty-one-year-old in the mirror. This woman is different than the woman a year ago. She is no longer broken. Michelle stands straight and looks intently at her reflection. *You are strong. You are loved.*

She leaves the restroom and glances toward the bar stool where her mom sat just moments ago. *She's gone.* Michelle breathes a sigh of relief and walks around the bar toward the room where her family and friends are gathered. She stops and stands in the doorway again, like she did when they first arrived. Taking in every second and watching her loved ones with an enormous amount of gratitude. *Everything I need is in this room.*